ALL
(WO)MEN
DESIRE
TO
KNOW

ALL
(WO)MEN
DESIRE
TO
KNOW

A Novel

by
Johanna Baldwin

Inspired by Dr. Raymond Moody's course *Wisdom Lovers*

FOREWORD & AFTERWORD
by Raymond A. Moody, Jr. M.D., Ph.D.

LISA HAGAN BOOKS

[handwritten inscription:] For Barbara — Friend + Goddess with love, Johanna B.

For RS3

"Fiction writers tell a different kind of truth."

—ARISTOTLE (384 BC–322 BC)

FOREWORD

*"Humankind, fleet of life like tree leaves, unsubstantial
as shadows, weak creatures of clay, wingless, ephemeral,
sorrow-worn, and dreamlike."*
　　　　　　　　—ARISTOPHANES (446 BC–388 BC)

JOHANNA BALDWIN'S TALE of love and
logic beautifully evokes the mysterious world of ancient
Greek philosophers. Her book's intriguing characters
are apt to feel strangely familiar to today's readers. That
is because all of us carry them around with us in our
hearts and minds without being able to put definite
names to them.

Sadly, men like Pythagoras, Parmenides, Socrates,
Plato, and Aristotle have mostly been brushed aside in
the modern world. Political correctness forbids us to
acknowledge that early Greek philosophers laid the
foundations upon which the greater part of our knowledge about the universe was built. They also forged the
instruments of reason which we still use—albeit main-
ly unconsciously—to think logically about the problems of life. The characters in Ms. Baldwin's novella

succeeded so spectacularly in implanting themselves deeply into our minds that we have forgotten all about them—even their names!

In an odd way, their actual names have become irrelevant. Instead, the people portrayed in this book have in effect become parts of our brains that are necessary for living in complex societies. Ms. Baldwin's fiction brings these ancient men alive by retrieving them from the very depth of our souls. The scenes in her book have an intense, evocative, dreamlike quality precisely because we already know the characters very well—only we don't know that we know them. The characters have receded into the background by becoming vital parts of our mind that operate automatically. For example, we understand that numbers are an integral part of scientific reasoning without having to think about the fact that Pythagoras came up with that principle. Or, we reason about what to do about problems in our finances or relationships without having to think about the fact that Aristotle worked out the principles with which we are reasoning.

All (Wo)men Desire To Know works so well also because Ms. Baldwin ties these ancient philosophers in with grief, which is perhaps the most painful and profound human emotion. That is very appropriate, too. For the ancient Greek philosophers were the first people to apply reason to the mystery of life after death. They studied near-death experiences, debated the subject in the same way we do today, and wrote books meant to console people in their grief over the loss of loved ones.

In sum, Johanna Baldwin's *All (Wo)men Desire To Know* is a beautiful book. I hope it will make people more conscious of the ancient scholars who founded western civilization and whose works set out the principles by which we still think today. In a time in which fundamental western values are under assault, that would be a very hopeful and important development.

—Raymond A. Moody, Jr. M.D., Ph.D.
Anniston, Alabama

CHAPTER ONE

SHE HAD BEEN looking and looking, going on twenty minutes now. Or was it thirty? Not an enormous amount of time, but a waste of time to search for a mere pencil. An ordinary, number two lead, school-color-yellow with eraser. She knew very well it was there, somewhere. She had already looked under her manila files, regular sized and the legal ones, even the ones she cut into a smaller dimension that made sense for her months of receipts she hadn't organized. She looked amidst the clutter of her desktop drawer, under her computer equipment and then inside all the file cabinet drawers. Even the hanging files, she repeatedly looked inside each of them, even in between all the messed-up papers. She knew her pencil existed and was in fact there in her office because it had been there thirty minutes before. Or was it forty? In her hands, she had used it to pencil in a date in her calendar. Another dinner plan she probably wouldn't keep. She still kept a paper diary when everybody else she knew programmed their schedules onto their electronic devices. She also knew other people still used pencils and began to think through, who in her office might have one. Perhaps she should stop looking, it was most definitely a waste of time to look for something she may never find. Or, if and when she did find it, would it be too late? She began to look under her manila files again.

He had told her this would happen. The Grievance Counselor Man. Probably her age, he was probably also in his late thirties. He was attractive although she clearly was not attracted to him. She didn't expect that the man who would take care of her husband, would be remotely interesting from an exterior point of view, let alone an interior one. Even so, he was guidance-counseling her without her permission. Her technique whenever he crossed the line was to change the subject and ask him about himself.

"Why would anybody want to be in the funeral business?" she asked. "Dealing with death and bodies. Not to mention despair."

She never asked for a Grievance Counselor. He combined two unappealing careers into one: Funeral Master Slash Counselor. It was one thing to seek out a counselor, another to be forced without one's permission.

When he was a younger man The Counselor told her, he was lucky enough to find the love of his life. And she had found him. They were together for a while until the head-on collision where they had to pry her body out of the remains of what once was an automobile. She was extracted from metal and glass. By the time he arrived at the funeral home, her face had been stitched up so badly, she was unrecognizable. She was not only grossly disfigured, she was embalmed.

Looked nothing like her. Not her structure, not her color. Seeing what they did to her or what they didn't do, was when he decided that he would make sure that anyone whoever loved, any kind of love in any range or spectrum, no matter how long or how brief, that he would take care of beloved passed-away bodies and hold them, preserve them. Keep them as close to who and what they were until the time of burial or the time of cremation. So that the ones they loved would be able to grapple with the transition.

After he used the word transition, she got up the nerve to ask him, "Did you ever see her again?"

"Who?" he asked.

"The love of your life."

He shook his head, negative.

She then asked, "Do you believe you will see her again?"

"I believe I will, but I don't know."

She couldn't remember his name, only the trace of his funeral-counseling beard. Mostly brown with strands of gray, clean cut for a beard. He had darkened eyes, although what color they were was of no consequence. They were dark, or was it the way she experienced them and they were actually filled with light? He did lift her up a bit although she did not request upliftedness. He was giving her something she did not desire.

And then, he wasn't the one she was thinking about most of the time. It was another he. The subject of he was not an obsession, she knew that. It was a calling, not an obsession, she kept reminding herself. What was the line drawn between the two? A quest, an obsession, a hope. Some people say hope is another version of obsession—it keeps you away from the present moment.

Her present moment and all moments that followed and all moments from his exact time of death came down to one thing. One simple question: Would she ever see him again?

Because if she didn't know she would ever see him again, she pretty much felt, or believed, that life just wasn't worth finishing the journey. What would the point be if you don't see the most sacred person in your life ever again? The person who gets you, who understands you, the person who accepts you, the person who sees beyond your flaws, the person who touches you in places you didn't even know about. The place where human and spiritual emotion reside together. And you get him too. You see his dreams and you experience his joyful visions being realized. And when he falls, you fall almost as hard if not harder than he does. You are so close that you anticipate each other's moods. And needs. You do not take ever, you give. And the two givers, for whatever reason, end up with an experience that creates a unified current between the two. Whether in the same city, whether in the same bed, whether in the same dream. And there is that connection that you never dreamed possible. You might have imagined something else, but not this dream. And instead of a dream, it is reality. A reality that no one had told you of before. Even the poets from the beginning of time seemed to end on tragedy when it came to true love. But they never called it true love, they called it real love. And real love has reality to it. Colds, bruises, misunderstandings, accidental hurt. Never direct bold-faced hurt. Doubt was very rare, but it cropped up every once in a while. Nobody had counted on her before and she had never counted on anyone. Such easy words to say, but to actualize them. He taught her that. "Count on me," he used to say. He made her say it out loud until she understood what it meant.

She didn't even know she was capable of love before. All her life she had conjured it up in her head. Whatever was missing with her other lovers, she would fill up the gap in some creative or imaginary way, so that she could experience love. Or a pale rendering of it. "Mind The Gap," they say of The London Underground or Tube. She would fill the gap with her lovers with whatever resources she could. Fill the gap. She was good at that. Whatever it took, she would fill it. Not enough trust, she would invent trust. Not enough caring, she would imagine deep caring. Not fulfilled sexually, she had a private way of minding that gap too.

But then when he came into her life, there was no gap to fill. He gave her everything she never knew about. And not with things or possessions. There were no rings, no vows, no contracts, no property, no joint bank accounts. But what was hers was his and what was his was hers. They knew this without ever speaking about it. It just was. Whatever the other needed was given without having to ask. There were no questions.

Why wouldn't she want to see him again? How could she go on? The only way she could go on was by knowing that she would see him again. She had to know. Without that, she didn't think she would make it. She knew she wouldn't.

The Funeral Master Slash Grievance Counselor Man told her that it takes two years to get over the death of a loved one. She was sure he didn't know what he was talking about. How can the question of losing real love have a mathematical answer?

She knew people came and went in one's life without any jurisdiction over what will happen tomorrow. Nobody knows. Everybody knows that after life follows death. But nobody knows what follows death. People say they know, but they don't. She wanted to know. No, she had to know.

Will I ever see him again?

She had already begun a practice of choosing whom to pose this question to. It didn't matter whether she knew the person well or not. Or, if she knew them at all. It could be a complete stranger. It was a screening process, meticulous, of whomever she came in contact with. Whoever it turned out to be, she would carefully listen to what that person had to say first. She might offer compassion or, if she had one, a solution. Based on this exchange, she would gage whether the person was a candidate for her question. Did they seem open, interested, experienced, enlightened? And then, if there were a pale glimmer of any of these qualities, she would ask as carefully as she could, without any trace of obsession or sadness or loss, did they think she would ever see him again?

She could sometimes feel other people's judgments after she asked the question. A shift in body language or facial expressions might indicate she was being viewed as weak or lost. Sometimes other people's judgments came off tenderly. Sometimes not. The atheists were by far the toughest. But she understood and silently forgave them. She wondered if they had silently forgiven her for holding a different opinion. In any case, she didn't want an opinion, she wanted the truth. And nothing less.

She knew she had to be discreet about her preoccupation. And she knew that she would spend the rest of her life with this one question until she knew.

Will I ever see him again?

She knew people might think she was selfish. But she knew it was not selfish at all because if it were true, if it were a fact, that she would see him again, that meant that others, all others, would have the same possibility. And that this new world would be the one worth living in, not the world where everything has an ending. That everybody had the chance to see his or her loved ones. Not in a puffy clouds and gated type of way, but in a real way where real love comes from.

Someone was tapping at her door. Another staff meeting was about to start. She asked her colleague if he had a pencil. He handed her a pen. She wrote in blue ink a name on a date and closed her diary. Then she stood up, grabbing her clipboard when her number two lead pencil dropped to the floor. It had been sitting right in front of her, on top of her clipboard, the whole time. She bent down to pick it up. Forty-five minutes must have gone by. Or was it an hour?

CHAPTER TWO

A LIGHT RAIN was coming down and it was a
relief because it had been pouring for a full day and
a half. She was a few minutes early for someone she
wasn't sure would even show up. Some Female Tourist
found her wallet in the back of a taxi and had plucked
her business card out and called her. She hadn't even
noticed she'd lost her wallet until the call came in.

She figured the Female Tourist must come to
New York regularly because she wanted to meet at The
Strand. Not every tourist knew about the bookstore
where you can buy an old book for a dollar as well as
pick up a brand new hard back at a decent price. The
store had a sophisticated bohemian vibe to it, although
New York has lost almost all its bohemian qualities.
Can't blame New York for that, the old bohemian New
York was when one would almost never get their wallet
back. Now in the new New York era, it was the consen-
sus, if you lost something in a taxi, there was a greater chance whatever it was would be returned, rather
than not returned. As long as whatever one lost was
traceable. Umbrellas were not traceable; she wondered

where all the lost umbrellas were in New York. Was there a place for them? Was there a place for lost people? But then she remembered that's what New York was to her. The city of lost people at one time. But once they were in New York and they had accepted New York and New York had accepted them, they became not found, but no longer lost.

He and she had shared this love for New York. They sometimes argued with each other, which was better? To be a born and raised New Yorker? Always—all your life knowing about New York and having the privilege of living there. Being from there was considered the highest pedigree of being a New Yorker. Or was it the second, never having seen New York before and then eventually discovering it? Discovering New York and moving to New York and New York embracing you enough to believe it can work and then the ultimate in making it work. Both options of either being a born New Yorker or becoming a New Yorker were two of the best things that could happen to a person. Outside of discovering Real Love. Real Love didn't have to happen in New York City. Finding Real Love did not require geography. But if it did have geography, and well, if you fell in love in New York, you pretty much were two of the luckiest people in the world. And they were.

She looked up and down Broadway and then looked across East 12th Street wondering of all the female tourists coming and going, which one of them would it be. She then wondered how much money she would give the Female Tourist. What was the price of being a Good Samaritan these days? Fifty or a hundred dollars? And then how much cash did she have in her wallet, or was there any cash left at all. Who was the Female Tourist really and would she really show up? And then she felt a hand touch her shoulder.

The Tourist stood under an umbrella wearing a fine suit of beige. She was maybe fifty, blond hair with some kind of old-fashioned hairspray on top. She could pass as a New Yorker; maybe she had been at one time. The Tourist handed her the lost wallet.

She said thank you before opening it, extracting whatever bills she could find, but The Tourist stopped her, explaining that she didn't need money, and she had planned on getting to The Strand anyway.

But then The Tourist said, "I'd be open to a free coffee. I'm always open for that."

The Tourist placed her umbrella above the both of them. A little too much intimacy she felt, why couldn't she run away now that she had her wallet back rather than having to strike a conversation with a person she didn't know. Her friends could barely get her out of the house. And now a tourist who returned her wallet was offering some protection she didn't want. She would rather just let the rain soak her hair and skin, but then suddenly The Tourist was pulling her down Broadway and then towards University Place into a Dean & Deluca annex. It was while crossing the street, she decided she wouldn't ask The Tourist her question. She didn't know exactly why she wouldn't ask, other than she was feeling agitated by the strange woman. She knew she wouldn't be tempted to ask, not this time.

The good thing about most tourists is that you don't need to do much to get along with them. All you need to do is to inquire as to where they're from and then typically a monologue begins. And so she sat, barely touching her black coffee while listening to The Tourist speak while taking measured gulps from her double-cappuccino. The Tourist was a professor at Indiana University, she held two PhDs of some kind. "My husband and I are both professors but he couldn't make this trip. We've been married for twenty years. And believe it or not, most of the time, happy. I wish he were here."

She understood more than The Tourist could know, about wishing an absentee husband were no longer absent. That said, she thought it was deeply self-centered The Tourist would brag about her twenty-year marriage. Didn't she realize most people never make it to happiness, and one should never gloat over such an accomplishment? It's a victory so few people ever have.

The Tourist continued, "As my husband couldn't come on this trip, I went on my own on a private tour below The Met where there is a basement full of rarely seen antiquities down there, very few people know about or have access to." The Tourist's voice faded from time to time, or probably it was that her interest level was waning. Evidently there was a whole world of private possessions below the museum, but you had to know somebody at the highest level, to get to the lowest level. The Tourist continued, " Just think I was observing someone else's uncovered treasures from thousands of years ago in a museum and then discovered your lost treasure in a taxi."

And then there was a lull in the conversation. She couldn't pretend she cared about what The Tourist was saying at all. Not until The Tourist asked the unexpected question. Not all questions are unexpected but this one definitely was.

"Why did you lose your wallet?" The Tourist inquired.

"What do you mean why?"

"We always lose things for a reason. It signifies your mind was or is somewhere else. Where was it? What were you thinking about?" The Tourist probed.

But she didn't answer, she just couldn't.

The Tourist then asked even more significantly, "Or. Did you lose someone?"

She couldn't even look in The Tourist's direction anymore. How invasive the woman was turning out to be. She did not know how to answer. Or maybe she didn't want to. Odd since the subject of he was on her mind just about every moment of every day and every night.

The Tourist spoke again, "I'm sorry, am I being too pushy? My husband tells me I sometimes am."

It got fairly quiet except for the espresso machines in the background and other people's conversations, whether customers or employees, had blended together into one familiar sound without intonation or culture. The sound of being anywhere in the world, anywhere where expensive coffees were sold. The Tourist withstood the silence between them and then asked with the softest tone she could manage, "Who was it?"

She finally answered, "My husband. But we weren't together twenty years, we were only together for two."

The Tourist then asked although she knew, "And he was it, right?"

Her answer, "How can you go on if the best thing that will ever happen to you has already happened?"

The Tourist knew better, "But that's not what's bothering you exactly, I mean it's something more challenging than that?"

The Tourist was onto her, she thought. How could a total stranger know something that her friends didn't even know or want to know about? It was all so strange, this random encounter. In one moment she resented The Tourist, and then a split moment later, she was grateful for her. Even so, she felt comfortable enough, or safe enough, to say it out loud again, and was it still a question or was it now a lifelong affirmation. She felt The Tourist already knew what she was going to say, but she said it aloud once again, "All I want to know is, will I ever see him again?"

Without thinking too much about it, The Tourist answered quickly, maybe too quickly. "Of course you will, if he was it, then you will. If he was not it, then I wouldn't be able to say for sure. But yes, you will."

She looked at The Tourist. "I believe it, but I want to know it. How is it that you know?"

The Tourist then became a bit agitated herself. "You know, New Yorkers have this kind of pride, whether it is true or not, about being the most sophisticated people in the world, but the truth is, you're not. You're far from not."

"I'm sorry, I don't know what you're talking about. My husband died, all I want to know or to be assured is that I will see him again because if I don't…"

The Tourist interrupted her this time, "I'm telling you, you will. Isn't that enough now to go on?"

It was not enough for The Tourist, pleasant or not, to tell her what she wanted to hear. She knew she had to know. Didn't the scholarly woman understand that?

The Tourist sighed before she told her the following, "Well, the truth is, it's Aristotle's fault."

She was confused again, "Aristotle? The Aristotle?"

"There was only one Aristotle, he was brilliant as I assume you know, but he had one flaw." The Tourist waited for her to ask her about his one flaw, but she sat quietly perplexed. The Tourist went on as if she were interested, "He overlooked the magic of the universe. He only believed in what was concrete. If he had believed like all the men that came before him..."

But she interrupted this time, in defense of her feminine side, "And what about the women that came before him?"

The Tourist defended herself, "The originators of western thought were men, and yes, women inspired and guided them, but they, men, were the ones who got credit for it. Or in Aristotle's case, discredited for it. Because before Aristotle, all men not only believed in magic, they knew about magic. Meaning, knew about life after death, knew about God or Gods as the case may be. They did not believe in Gods, they knew their Gods. They had their own personal relationships with them and would do just about anything to be close to the source. All of them, each brilliant man since 550 BCE up until the time of Aristotle knew what you want to know. From Pythagoras, to Xeonophanes, to Heraclitus, to Parmenides, to Zeno, to Empedocles, to Anaxagoras, to Democritus, to Socrates, to Antisthenes, to Plato, until Aristotle and even after Aristotle there was Menippus."

She tried to stop her a couple of times, but The Tourist did not hear her voice until she finished rattling off her list of the Great Thinkers. All just The Tourist's opinion, of course. Most of the Thinkers she had never heard of before and basically could hardly have cared less. Who cares about the Greeks, anyway? Or history. Or someone else's relics. All she wanted was to see her husband again and not to be lectured or harassed by a Tourist even if she could have passed for a New Yorker earlier in the day. She focused on putting her guard up again, the one that The Tourist was trying to tear down. She was finally able to break through The Tourist's lecture, when she began one of her own.

"Listen, I appreciate your knowledgeable words, even the ones that are over my head including the names of men I'll never remember. You are a PhD intellectual who lives in a university setting and has all the time in the world to contemplate the meaning of history and such. That's what you do; you have the great fortune to live in that isolated world. I, however, live in a real world, one where I'm devastated about the loss of my husband. And, none of what you said makes much difference to me. Please don't take offence, it's as if we are speaking in different languages. You are speaking historical Greek; I am speaking modern day survival. I know you mean well."

The Tourist became abrasive. "I don't mean well. I mean. If you want to know without question that you will see your husband again, the only way is to go back to the origins of Western Thought, back to Greece, back to 600–320 BCE, and there you will find your answer. No one can tell you otherwise. No priest, no rabbi, no shrink, no scholar, no shaman, no best friend, no enemy, no stranger. Because with all those avenues you are merely entertaining a belief system. If it weren't for Aristotle, it's quite possible, if not probable, that you would know you would see him again. You would not be lost, or be losing things, you would know. But then we wouldn't have had the chance to meet, would we? And I would not be the irritating tourist who brought you your lost wallet filled with shreds of paper and plastic that will not last an eternity, but only a few more years."

Her heart was racing, her breath had shortened. She wondered how she was going to get rid of The Tourist. Was The Tourist crazy, or was there the fragment of a chance she spoke any truth. It didn't matter what the answer was, all she wanted to do was get out of the situation she was in. How would she do it? How would she get rid of her? But The Tourist made the first move, "I am sorry you lost your husband and that you didn't get to have him for longer. But I am not sorry to offer you an insight into the only truth. No one can tell you what you want to know, you have to find out for yourself. On your own. You have to learn this on your own, because you'll see, nobody but nobody will understand what you are going through, let alone understand what you truly need. Your friends and people who care for you will be interested for as long as they can be because they, too, are going through things you do not understand. Things they probably haven't even told you about out of respect for the passing of your husband. I highly recommend you go as far as you have to go to find the answer you are looking for, otherwise, you'll keep losing things that have no meaning. Until then, you'll be looking for the temporary losses as a distraction, or a barrier to stand in the way of what you truly want. And we both know what you truly want and need. And your needs, by the way, are everyone's needs, because we all need to know. What if belief were someday a thing of the past and instead we knew?"

Before she could think of an answer, The Tourist was gone and it was no longer raining outside. Though inside it was starting to rain. In fact the storm was emerging from within now. Her eyes were full, as her private rain began to stream down her face. A young man with a shaved head seated at the next table tried to brighten her mood when he asked, "Was that your aunty?"

No, she said, "Just another tourist."

The Shaved-Headed Young Man handed her some napkins so she could wipe her tears. As she took them, she glanced outside and saw the sunlight reflecting from the drenched streets and buildings magnifying the glory of another New York day. She wished he could see it. She longed for him to see it.

When she stepped outside, she looked up and down the golden, mirrored streets. There were more tourists everywhere, but she didn't recognize a one. As she walked away from the annex, she did not notice The Tourist's umbrella had been left behind, leaning against their empty table. Another lost umbrella. The city was filled with them. At least this one was not hers.

CHAPTER THREE

SHE WAS LYING unclothed on the couch under several comforters unable to sleep. Again. There was a bed in the next room. She didn't avoid going into the bedroom, she just couldn't lie down on the bed. Their bed. She tried to sit on the mattress a couple of times, but that's as far as she could go. She would never sleep on their bed again, but she couldn't get rid of it either. Not yet. Or maybe not ever. She wondered what other lovers did when their real loves were never going to return. What about those beds? What about all those bedrooms? Did everybody leave his or her former bedrooms and homes or did everybody stay. Which was better? What did other lovers do, she wondered. Were all abandoned lovers awake at night? Were all abandoned lovers wondering the same thing, were they all lying awake on their couches?

They had made love on the couch, of course. Like most lovers do. But couch love was always a prelude to something else. No matter what sexual activity occurred in any corner of their home, whether lying down, standing up, leaning, sitting, right side up or upside down, grasping, caressing, crawling, eyes open or eyes closed, they always ended it in each other's arms in bed. It was not an elaborate bed or bedroom. They always spoke about getting a new bed, one that didn't have squeaky springs or wheels, one where the neighbors might not get too annoyed. She wondered if her neighbors were happy her bedroom no longer had sounds emanating through the walls. She sure never liked to hear other people having sex, but when it came to them, they couldn't help themselves. They didn't want to help themselves. They made love as if it were their last day on earth. Every single time, even if it was one of the fast versions, it was as if it were their last day on earth together. Until one day it was.

She was tired of remembering things, she wanted to be active in her life not just in her mind. When he was alive, she was active and it was not only about him. He, she, they had work they cared about, they had a community of friends they cared about, they had their families they cared about. After they met, after they began to know they were made for each other, her heart began to expand rather than contract. With all other lovers who came before, she had a restrictive place in her heart when it came to love. As if a net were cast and whenever the lover got too far away, whether it was physical distance or emotional distance, her heart would constrict. With these other former lovers, there were threatening sensations that would cause her heart to palpitate differently. She had thought these overactive palpitations were an indication of love. He had opened her up and he had said the same thing about her.

Neither one of them knew about this enlargening

of the human heart before. These hearts that seemed to grow wider and taller were not lavished solely on each other. Wherever their oversized hearts were, together or separate, they were capable of more love for others too. And not only reserved for loved ones. Easy to love loved ones. But there was an extra measure of love for colleagues and neighbors whether they were fond of them or not, for local sellers in markets or on the streets. More love for doormen, for postal workers, more for nurses and doctors and receptionists. More for the poor. More for the rich whether the good kind of wealth or the hideous kind. More tenderness for trash collectors and tax collectors. They were able to conjure up compassion for fraudulent businessmen and businesswomen. There was acceptance of bad drivers and telephone salespeople who called at untimely hours. They were able to uncover humane thoughts for the politicians who were bringing harm to society. Far from perfect, these expansive hearts were. And they were well aware of that fact. They were not immune to disappointment, frustration or hurt of any kind. They felt pain like anyone else. But these two enlivened hearts functioned with the best of intentions, whether successful or unsuccessful. This kind of love was utterly new to the both of them. There was, they agreed, enough to go around for everyone.

She wanted her overly large heart back, so that she could be a part of whatever world was left for her. Now, her heart wasn't enormous nor was it constricted. It was numb. Emotion, of any sort, no longer held jurisdiction in her heart. Whatever happened, it would feel just about the same just about all the time. Her heart was frozen and yet she wasn't cold.

She tried to think of other things, and sometimes would do breathing exercises, to think of no things. Her healer friend had told her, breathe deeply, four breaths in and four breaths out until your energy shifts. Something about meridians. It did work sometimes, but then most times, it would just make her feel more faint. The only other thing she could think about, quite strangely, was The Tourist, as irritating as she was. Not that she wanted to think about her. But The Tourist was starting to recur in her mind, unwanted. The bland and beige of the whole incident. The rain. The umbrella. The lecture. The only color that afternoon occurred under The Strand's red awning before The Tourist even got there. And yet, overriding all these details, it was The Tourist's Aristotle reference that was recurring in her thoughts. Why was she subjected to thinking about the ridiculous opinions of one tourist? And, Aristotle of all people.

Again she tried her best to think of other things and again she tried the meridian breathing for a while. Four breaths in, four breaths out. But the image of The Tourist kept coming back. The Tourist *and* Aristotle were becoming embedded in her thoughts. She was not numb when she thought of them, nor was her heart expansive.

The only thing she could think to do at this point was to reach for her laptop. Millions of people use computers as an escape, why shouldn't she? She glanced past her virtual mailbox of unread messages, instead navigating over to her search bar. She hesitated at first, she breathed in and breathed out a few more times and then she typed onto her computer screen: Aristotle's Fault.

There was much, too much information. There were thousands of studies, references and quotes about Aristotle from all countries of the world. From all major cities as well as more remote places. Harare, Zimbabwe—Olathe, Kansas—many towns she had never heard of, there were five villages just in New Zealand let alone the larger continents. It went on and on and on, pages and pages and pages. Many of the sites were in languages and dialects she had never heard of. And nothing specifically about what The Tourist told her. Nothing she could find. There was so much other information however, it was almost as debilitating as her inner struggle. She tried breathing and searching and wondered why so many people, so many cultures cared at all about this Thinker, great or not, Aristotle.

She clicked on and off sites and pages mindlessly until she realized she was starting to get tired. A relief she thought. Maybe researching history she didn't care about would be her new way of getting to sleep sooner. Better than a prescription or arduous phone calls from friends trying to help. And then she came across something Aristotle was to have said. It was only one sentence, but it stuck with her.

Aristotle's sentence read, "All men by nature desire to know."

She didn't expect a man who she would never meet, who died thousands of years ago from a country she had never been to nor was interested in going to, could know how she felt. She stared at the screen, taken aback by an unexpected emotion. She kept staring at his seven words: "All men by nature desire to know." She then decided to highlight his words and then she cut and pasted them onto a document of her own. She added two letters to his quote, although his quote would retain his simple seven words.

And then she said it out loud in the middle of the night, "All women by nature desire to know." But no one could hear.

While staring at these seven words on her screen, her eyes became glossy. And yet this time, there was no weeping. The sentence on her laptop stayed illuminated for a while, until her computer screen fell asleep. *All women by nature desire to know,* she thought over and over again. Until, she too, finally fell asleep.

CHAPTER FOUR

SHE STARED UP at the tall staircase, daunted. More tourists, but there were intellectuals and students and an older set too. Another New York blessing. Everybody fit in. Even the craziest looking person you'd ever seen, moments later would no longer be the craziest looking person you'd ever seen because someone else had come along to become the craziest looking person you'd ever seen. And you'd hardly notice anyway, because of the coming together of so many different types of persons: Crazy looking or sane looking, along with the scale of human stature measured in feet, inches and pounds, not to mention the unique shades of everyone's skin tones including hair textures and colorings, plus any special markings whether born-with or imposed. All these variances amongst the clusters of people held a unifying quality.

She knew very well she could enter the marble structure and simply blend in. And the best thing about it would be that no one would know she had lost a thing. The anonymity of being a New Yorker. The thought gave her the courage to climb the cement steps.

After the long line and security check, the guards let her through. She took the circular staircase up to the third floor and then moved through the North Hall. The Rose Main Reading Room had a divine quality, whether or not whoever entered had belief in divinity. *Belief.* That's why she had come, she wanted more than belief. She needed more.

While searching through the computer catalog, she wasn't surprised there were, once again, too many choices. After turning in her first series of call slips, she located the three sets of shelves filled with green-bound books. The words of the Greek Thinkers were housed here, but it was at eye level, at Section 121, where one row solely focused on The Thinker she was interested in—whether written by or all about Aristotle.

She selected Seat Number 213 so she would be close to the green books and keep an eye on the delivery desk. She didn't want to waste too much time on this inexplicable endeavor, but she was curious. After all, Aristotle had helped her fall asleep for more than one night.

Before opening the Thinker's first volume, she found herself distracted by all the different types of people in the midtown library. She could pretty much tell which ones were regulars, authentic intelligentsia, and which ones were the fakes. Or dabblers. She figured the regulars could detect the dabblers from the tourists and the tourists from the fakers without having to look up. Most people's minds were buried in their books or onto their computer screens. She wondered what everyone was searching for.

It was fairly quiet, although there was the low-grade hum of all the multi-languaged whispering. She noticed natural light seeping in from the high windows above, even with all the scaffolding. Her eyes took in the painted ceiling—a pale blue sky and puffy clouds the color of rose. Angels were plentiful, as were elaborate chandeliers. There were rows of long oak tables, immaculately polished with bronze lamps.

Sitting at one of those tables, she thus began turning Aristotle's pages without distraction. She read each page slowly at first, but not long after began to turn the pages more quickly. Glancing, scanning for any clue of what The Tourist mentioned to her and then she began more rapid page turns. One page after the next, more searching than reading. Every time she picked up books from the delivery desk, she filled out more call slips. More page turning, more books, more call slips. One book after the next, searching and wanting. She was on a mission to find one true thing and one true thing only. She wasn't interested in becoming another Aristotle follower, she just wanted to know. She wanted to know about Real Love and would she ever have access to it again. *Would she ever see him again?* Nothing in these books had helped her so far, but somehow Aristotle kept encouraging her to go on. She could almost hear the sound of The Thinker's voice: *All women by nature desire to know.*

Midway between returning excessive amounts of books and turning in more call slips, she was intercepted by a tall and lean young man who was rather smart looking. He asked, "Looking for something?"

"Of course I am. Why would I be here otherwise?"

He handed her additional books she had

requested and walked away without a response.

She followed him, whispering too loudly, "I'm sorry—I didn't realize you worked here. Please forgive me."

"Do you need help or not?"

"Yes, I do. Do you know anything on the subject having to do with…Aristotle's Fault? Or could you refer me to any person or any periodical that might be able to help me? "

"Nope, I'm not into Greek history. Never was." And then he went behind the librarian's counter.

She persisted, "Is there anybody here who is into Greek history?"

"Well, Jaros was pretty knowledgeable, but he's not here anymore."

"Did he go to another branch by any chance? Can he be reached?"

"Nope, he went to Greece. Nobody's heard from him since. Can you imagine, being so obsessed with a subject, you just get up one morning and leave your job and buy a one way ticket and nobody ever hears from you again?" The Smart Looking Young Man turned his back to her and began to help another information seeker.

She returned to her Seat Number 213 wondering what the former librarian Jaros was doing in Greece and if he was happy there.

The next time she looked up, there was no longer natural light coming from above, the real sky had darkened and so had the reading room. The regulars were still there, but most of the crowd had filtered out. The multi-languaged whispering was quieter than before. She observed the regulars who were still buried in their research. She wondered again, what everybody was looking for. Was everyone depending on one single answer to their own one single question that would enable them to go on? Whether to graduate from a certain school, whether to find a line of poetry that would change their lives, whether to find the cure for an illness, whether to change science, whether to change politics. Did everybody else have one question, and one question only, they had to know the answer to?

She hadn't remembered writing anything down, but when she looked at her spiral pad, she saw her very own hand-written notes. None of it legible except another quote from The Thinker: *All human actions have one or more of these seven causes: chance, nature, compulsions, habit, reason, passion, desire.*

Then, the regulars began to put their computers and notes away. They were returning their journals and books. She took their cue and returned the green books back to their home. She touched them gently before leaving them. She then took her requested books back to the librarian's counter. The Smart Looking Young Man was no longer there.

Spiraling down the staircase with the regulars, she felt no sense of accomplishment or victory from any of the women and men she had just spent an entire day and most of an evening with. There were no personal exchanges, or glances. Once they all got outside, they all went their separate ways. Within moments all the regulars disappeared into the New York night without a trace. Lingering on the steps, she wondered what she was doing there and why she felt so incomplete. She glanced again at her note pad, but was thinking about the former librarian who fled to Greece. And then she discarded all her research, her entire note pad, into a recycling container. After which, she descended down to Fifth Avenue, blending into the nighttime maze, vanishing like all the regulars.

CHAPTER FIVE

SHE DECIDED SHE would say yes. It had been awhile since she had agreed. Even when he was still alive, she never really wanted to go. Drinks with colleagues and friends. She did enjoy a glass of champagne on occasion, and on other occasions she might indulge in something stronger. But not in groups of people. For her, lonely experiences seemed to occur while in a bar or at a cocktail party. A drink over dinner was one thing. Yet to go out to drink for drinking's sake was hardly appealing. Fragments of conversations, fragments of ideas—nothing too meaningful, not too deep. However on this occasion, she thought it might be a good change. Reentry into a life without him—*with anesthesia*. She wouldn't go to escape the idea of having lost Real Love. She would go simply to do something. Anything other than to have thoughts seep in about The Tourist or The Thinker. Moreover, anything other than to ask herself or another, *will I ever see him again?* As true and as real as her quest was, it had become exhausting. She figured drinks with colleagues and friends might diffuse their perceptions about how much she thought about him. She knew she wouldn't bring up the most important thing she cared about in a group over cocktails in a loud bar. It would be ludicrous to shout one's truest desires across the laps of drinkers.

And it wasn't as bad as she thought. The loud music was less invasive than she expected and the people weren't so loud either. The secretary with no other aspirations other than to be a good secretary, had gone ahead early enough to get a corner table with plenty of extra chairs. The Good Secretary pointed out to her, "If you turn your head at just the right angle, you can see a clear slice of the Hudson River."

She could see the Good Secretary regretting the mention of the river immediately.

"I'm sorry," was all the Good Secretary could think of to say.

There was nothing either of them could do about it. She didn't look out at what would be the glittering Hudson as the sun was exiting for the day. The Hudson River used to have special powers at any time. It used to be a spectacular sight. But now, she never wanted to look at the Hudson River ever again.

She told the Good Secretary not to worry about it, "The Hudson River will be there long after we're all gone."

Several of her colleagues were already finishing their first rounds and her Boss was only a few minutes late, which was a positive considering he hardly ever showed up to these things. Unsurprisingly her Boss had brought along his younger Number One Assistant, who carried his streak of ruthlessness with transparency. And her Boss also brought a friend, a Guy in a

Baseball Cap. It was unlike her Boss to bring someone from his private life because as friendly as he was, he had clear boundaries between being the Boss and all the others who worked for him. Her Boss introduced the Guy in the Baseball Cap, but his name slipped her mind before he shook her hand.

The first couple of sips of vodka were rough, then smooth. As the liquid went down, her throat and then her face slowly became warm. The Guy in the Baseball Cap was kind and friendly. He was attentive, he talked about his cat by name, Ginger, and showed her multiple pictures of the feline he had taken on his cell phone. Everything was becoming warm she realized. She liked the feeling the drink was gifting her. It was as if she were taking a break from the importance of the true quest ahead of her. Everything was on hold, if just for a couple of hours. She was attempting to live in the present moment, as the Buddhists do, meditating, albeit with a large glass of alcohol in hand.

She found herself laughing for the first time she could remember. It was genuine, or so it seemed. And the tacky, shiny bar shades of red and black, as well as the mirrored and chromed room had become less tacky. Women with anxious faces were becoming beautiful. Men with predatory eyes were becoming handsome. The thumping sound called music pulsated, and what rattled inside her before was becoming rhythmic. All these things that normally irritated her to the point of refusing on most occasions to go out for drinks with colleagues and friends, was becoming accessible and inviting. She began to talk about the next time they would all go out together to alternative watering holes. She didn't have to order another drink, one appeared in front of her as if she were in a dream. The perfect measure of vodka, tonic and a twist of lemon. The halter-topped Female Bartender had sent her confidence in a chilled glass. She took the glass and drank the second much faster than the first and soon noticed that the Guy in the Baseball Cap was sitting closer to her than before. He was asking her things about herself, where she grew up and why didn't she have a pet? She appreciated that he avoided the subject that he must have heard about, the subject of how she lost her Real Love. She appreciated him.

A mild spinning had begun in her head; she wasn't drunk but she was intoxicated. Was there a difference, she thought for sure there must be. Drunk sounded pathetic, while intoxicated sounded less harsh. Intoxicated sounded socially acceptable. It didn't register at first, but her head spun around more when she saw that the Guy in the Baseball Cap was looking at her in that way. The way that men look when they want more. Then it dawned on her—her Boss had brought the Guy in the Baseball Cap to meet her as a set up. Now she was much warmer than before, not from wanting but from embarrassment. If she were a normal woman, with normal desires, she would probably have been pleased to meet him or flattered. Possibly thrilled, as he was as handsome as all the guys she liked when she was at school. He was as kind. He was as warm. He made her laugh a bit. And, he had a cat named Ginger. He held all the elements of a potential lover if she were looking for a lover. Before she met her Real Love, the Guy in the Baseball Cap could have been a candidate because before she met her Real Love, she didn't know better. She had thought a nice man with nice eyes with a nice demeanor with a sexual edge was enough. Maybe for a few nights it was plenty. But after finding out what Real Love was—a real soul connection, a real mind connection, a real erotic connection—there was hardly anything another man could do. Even if Real Love was gone, even if Real Love had gone to the other side of life. Gone to the place most people call death. She despised that word. Death. It was an unattractive word and it sounded so permanent. And here she was drinking for drinking's sake, sitting next to a Guy in a Baseball Cap who was trying his best to cheer her up and maybe or eventually trying to get her to bed. Unfortunately for the both of them, what he really turned out to be doing was highlighting what was missing in her life. Rather than escaping the longing for her Real Love, the Guy in the Cap was the catalyst emphasizing her longing, emphasizing her true needs, emphasizing her true desires.

Worse, much worse, than the Guy in the Baseball Cap, and she wasn't sure whether it was the alcohol or a calling or imagined, she was starting to hear voices in her head. First, it was The Tourist's voice, "If you want to know without question that you will see your husband again, the only way is to go back to the origins of Western Thought, back to Greece, back to 600-320 BCE, and there you will find your answer."

And then it was The Thinker's Voice. All his theories and quotes she didn't comprehend the day she spent in the library, all the spiral-padded notes she threw out that day, flooded her head. And then she heard Aristotle say, "All human actions have one or more of these seven causes: chance, nature, compulsions, habit, reason, passion, desire." Compulsion, passion and desire, weren't they all the same thing, she wondered. If The Thinker were there, she might very well ask him that. In fact, she would like to ask him that. She drained her second drink and began her third when The Tourist and The Thinker spoke together in unison: *"All women by nature desire to know."* Was it the alcohol, a calling or imagination talking to her, she wondered as her head spun around more. No, she wasn't drunk she told herself, she was overwhelmed. She privately tried inhaling four breaths in, four breaths out. Hard to do with in a public space with a spinning head. And a revolving room. She decided to try to stand up, ended up on the floor instead. Out cold.

CHAPTER SIX

SHE DIDN'T REMEMBER sleeping at all when she woke up in their bed. In that split second of possibility, between dreams and reality, she reached for him before the reminder of permanence came. He was no longer there. She turned away from his side of the bed and now faced their small abandoned terrace. Nothing but dead roses and plants outside her window.

And then the reminder of the night before came. How did she get home anyway? And then the taste of vodka came. She drank water down to fight the tide of stale alcohol, and the sour taste of lemon and club soda fought back. Waves of nausea followed, only to be joined by a series of dizzy spells. Her apartment walls and ceiling began to shift and spin. Each and every pore of her body was opening up—one by one—wounds in the making. A violence erupted inside her. She had to move quickly, in fact she ran.

She threw herself over the toilet, purging everything she had inside her. One retch, two retches. Her sickness spewed inside and outside the boundaries of the porcelain's rim. More and more retching, ongoing, debilitating, relentless. As she continued, she wondered, why was she so ill? She hadn't had that much to drink, had she? Too many drinks. Furious with herself, she tried to make it all go away by flushing down undissolved aspirins and discolored alcohol that were swimming in the water below. She wiped away the residual liquid and bile from her mouth and almost treasured a long moment of serenity. Her hands were shaking, and yet it was with these very hands she starting cleaning up after herself. First it was the floor. She tried wiping the evidence away until the dry heaves arrived. Involuntary spasms without vomit. Her throat, her eyes, her lips, her nose and her mouth became even more uncomfortably dry. On her now weak, empty stomach she leaned over again, gagging, her body demanding to expel the poison that was no longer there. Unwanted, uncomfortable throbbings radiated from head to toe, organs and orifices alike. Until another moment of serenity, this one she didn't trust. She waited and waited for the next eruption. She waited so long she didn't know how much time passed, until finally, she collapsed onto the bathroom floor. Overheated by toxins and self-manifested illness, she peeled off her clothes. Her naked skin on the cold tiles helped realign her equilibrium. More spasms rippled the length of her body as she lay there. She had nothing left to empty but emptiness itself.

It incensed her to think she hadn't moved forward. In fact, she had moved backward. Far backward. Lying naked on what was their bathroom floor, the only thing she knew was that she couldn't go on like this. She had to do something different about the whole thing. She knew she had to take a different approach to her new life. The new life that she didn't want or ask for. What could it be, what could she do differently that would somehow liberate her without having to sacrifice her true needs?

If she only knew for a fact she would see him again, she knew she could go on with her life without him. She could get through every single day and night if she knew. Maybe she could even flourish in an area of her life she hadn't embraced before. Maybe she would become more ambitious at work. Or maybe she would become a more generous volunteer. She hadn't volunteered for anything for quite some time. A friend at the free clinic had been asking her to spare a few hours a week. There were so many things one could volunteer to do in New York or anywhere. If she knew she would see him again, be with him again, she imagined the volunteer aspect in her heart that lay dormant could revive itself. No telling what other things she might do. Maybe take her grandmother on that road trip she'd been promising. Maybe she'd take piano lessons again. If she knew for a fact she would see him again, there were so many things she would do.

She also knew she didn't want to be on this earth moping around because of what was lacking. Lacking did no one any good. Everybody knows that. Anytime you see someone else focused on what they don't have, you can see their unhappiness, moreover you can feel it. She did not want to be the someone else filled with the disease of lacking. But how could she find her way out of this terrain, she speculated.

All she needed to know was that somehow, someday, some way, somewhere in a dimension she didn't fully understand they would connect again, however abstract, and if she knew that, she could sort out the pieces of her life and move on. She didn't see this way of thinking as delusional, as she wasn't expecting him to come back to life to pick up exactly where they left off—she knew that was an impossibility. She didn't want to live in a fantasy; she wanted to live in reality where everything makes sense, and beauty, true beauty, true love, Real Love never dies. And not based on memory. She didn't want to live in memory for memory can be a trap too. She wanted to live in the present and she wanted to know she would see him again, plain and simple. Certainly other people must be going through the same thing and what about all the people who came before. Anyone who has ever loved must have gone through this. Billions of people must all have wanted the same thing at one time or other. Mustn't they?

Exhausted by alcohol poisoning that she was solely responsible for and exhausted by over-contemplation that she also was equally responsible for, she made a deal with herself. Before the end of this very day, she would find a workable solution to her life's biggest and only true problem. She had no idea what the solution would be, but she made a commitment to herself to find another way to go on. Before the end of this day, she would know how to continue in a way she didn't know or understand now. She made this promise to herself quietly and then she said it out loud. "I will find a solution before the end of this day." And then she pulled herself off the bathroom floor.

CHAPTER SEVEN

SHE RESTARTED HER DAY by cooking a hangover breakfast of scrambled eggs, toast and black coffee. She felt a tinge of success in that although the eggs were overcooked and the toast was near-burnt, she had completed this task of cooking, eating and washing dishes without the obsession of Real Love. Plus, there were no thoughts whatsoever of The Tourist or The Thinker.

She took the bus into work rather than the subway. By choosing a different mode of transport, something she didn't ordinarily do, she hoped a simple act of change might jar her way of thinking. She wasn't expecting a miracle on the bus; she wasn't naïve. But she did think maybe, just maybe, a different way of getting somewhere might open up something inside of her. After all, that's what she was doing, she was committing to change and as small as the step was in taking the bus instead of the subway, she took it.

The Third Avenue Express moved slowly and the people on the bus moved slower than the people on the subway. An older, more eccentric group of riders seemed to be on the bus versus all the subway and taxi riders—hard to believe one mode of transportation could congregate more eclecticism than another. From bus stop to bus stop, the large Bus Driver sang out each stop from his diaphragm, overly loud, and not necessarily in tune. She didn't follow or recognize any of his melodies while he sang the names of 27th Street, 34th Street and upward. As refreshing as the change of transportation was, the bus was crawling along and it was going to make her late for work.

Ten blocks before her destination, she got out of the bus. Outside, on the sidewalks of the morning rush, she walked as fast as she could along the same route the bus took. The bus weaved in and out of traffic while she weaved in and out of strangers. She expected she would be able to move at a faster pace than the bus and she was mostly right. She was ahead most of time, though occasionally the bus would sail through a green traffic light or two enabling the singing driver and his bus to overtake her. But then when the driver was forced to stop for red lights or for exiting and incoming passengers, she would overtake him again. This went on for several exhilarating blocks, the blocks where she didn't consider anything else other than winning the race against the bus and getting to work on time. All this momentum continued until she and the Bus Driver both reached 50th Street at the exact same time, where they parted ways.

Breathlessness overcame her outside Rockefeller Center, while she headed towards the Atlas Building. She stole an extra thirty seconds to gather her wits, staring up at the massive seven-ton statue of the Greek Titan Atlas who forever holds heaven above his shoulders, and then she went inside.

From golden lobby to standard elevator to sterile hallway to corporate lobby to narrower hallway and into her small windowless office, her breathing had finally regulated itself. And nobody seemed to notice she was late. Waiting for her on her desk was a small, badly wrapped package in brown paper. Handwritten on the brown paper were different signatures from all her colleagues. She opened the package—finding a dozen brand new pencils and her very own brand new electronic pencil sharpener—so when she lost another pencil, she wouldn't have to look far for another one. The sound of the sharpener emanated through the thin office walls as she sharpened each of her new pencils. Thinking about her colleagues, and that they cared, lifted her spirits to a higher place. She hoped her own ability to care for others would reactivate soon.

She worked silently at her desk all morning without looking up. She didn't speak to a solitary person, she didn't lose a thing, she didn't take a break for a coffee, tea or to go to the ladies room. She didn't think about Real Love or contemplate the meaning of one thing, she simply worked. She added, she subtracted, she multiplied all morning long until she noticed it was well into lunchtime, and saw that most of the offices had emptied for lunch. She wasn't really hungry after her hangover breakfast and she hadn't forgotten about her new commitment to herself. In harsh terms, this commitment was nothing more than commanding herself to get a grip. She sat back and gave herself a quiet pat on the back for having worked an entire business morning without thinking of her Real Love.

The moment she acknowledged this small victory

to herself however, thoughts of Real Love swept back in, in the only way love can do. A sweeping joyous emotional circuitry of love, the kind that makes you want to stay in an ethereal phase forever. Once the strain of love came back, that meant thoughts of The Tourist were coming back too, as were thoughts of The Thinker. She sat incredibly still for a while, not knowing what to do next. Was she creeping back to the emotional state of no return, was she back on her bathroom floor? She could certainly combat it, she could fill up her day with lists of things to do, but that wasn't the point. The point was to arrive at her newfound commitment to herself without giving up what she wanted.

She understood why she was still over-thinking Real Love, but she didn't understand why she was still over-thinking The Tourist or Aristotle.

All women by nature desire to know.

The Tourist, she thought again and again.

She hesitated only for a moment, then reached toward her computer. She typed: Indiana University. And then hit return. The search was greater than she expected. There were eighteen hundred faculty and staff members that worked across eight campuses. Which campus had The Tourist mentioned, or did she tell her? There was a navigational tool entitled Find People Service, where she tried to locate The Tourist, but without remembering The Tourist's name, the online service did her no good. She didn't hesitate to reach for the phone.

As innocent as her question was, "Does anybody know the female professor there who teaches Western Thought or anything similar?" she didn't get the feedback she wanted, not even a scrap of information on

The Tourist. She tried explaining, "The professor, although I don't remember her name, helped me with my lost wallet and I wanted to thank her or to write to her." She also tried many other variations including, "I think she's married to another professor there, are there any married professors you could refer me to?" She always started with please and always ended in thank you. And yet, after trying all eight campuses and a handful of people per campus, they all told her the same thing: No one knew of such a woman, or professor, or married professors, past, present or future. It was a chilly reception, as all the responses, whether from men or women, were characteristically academic. She didn't sense any underlying passion or interest in the unknown that she remembered when she attended school those decades ago. And weren't universities supposedly built to aid curiosity and to seek truths and answers to the most complex questions?

She was angrier at herself than at all of the people she spoke to, combined. What the hell was she doing? What the hell was she thinking? Lost in her own thoughts, she didn't hear her Boss' Number One Assistant come in. He was cordial and didn't mention that he observed her talking to herself. He also didn't mention drinks with Colleagues the night before. It was awkward between them because they never had a rapport, as that was not one of his strengths. The only rapport he had was with his Boss and all superior work connected to his Boss. He was borderline cold, and strangely pleasant at the same time. The Boss' Number One Assistant asked if she would take a walk with him.

Of course, he knew that she knew that whenever

he took an employee for a walk, the employee would generally come back with a different position. And never a promotion because the Boss was the one who gave out the promotions. A different position given by the Boss' Number One Assistant was usually something more distant than the work the employee was previously doing. This is what they called a transfer. And then the other times, the employee might lose his or her position entirely, and you'd almost never see them again. She didn't expect she would be fired. If the love of her life hadn't died, she might deserve to be fired because all her office responsibilities were taking her longer than usual. Her weekly accountings and her monthly accountings had fallen behind. There had been errors in some of her billings, minor errors, but the wrong dates and sometimes the wrong amounts had shown up on several of the outgoing invoices she'd approved. Her work before she lost the love of her life was fairly impeccable. Some might say being an accountant is the most boring thing one can do with one's life. Yet when you have a full life outside of business hours, it's the best kind of job, because you don't take your problems home with you because rarely are there problems with numbers. Adding, subtracting, multiplying. How hard can it be if you're focused? But everybody in the office knew, including if not especially her Boss and her Boss' Number One Assistant, that her work was not what it used to be. And her numbers as simple as they were to calculate didn't quite, as the expression goes, add up.

They walked outside but didn't talk. She kept expecting to be lectured or scolded, as it was too quiet a walk. She wasn't all that nervous because the worst thing that could happen to her had already happened, so what could he possibly say or do that would make her sink deeper. On the other hand, she wasn't in the mood to lose her job.

He pulled her into one of the swank midtown hotels, whether it was The Peninsula or The Four Seasons, she couldn't remember as she hadn't even kept track of what street they were on. All she could remember was that he took her into a dark hotel bar to its furthest corner. It was the most comfortable leather barstool she ever sat on. He ordered her an expensive sandwich for her, but only ordered bottled water for himself.

Then he spoke without looking at her, "Everybody's worried about you."

She didn't know what to say, so she didn't say anything.

He repeated, "Everybody's worried about you."

She asked, "So what are we going to do about it?"

"Find a solution, what else?"

She liked the sound of the word solution coming from another person just as much as when she had said it to herself. Because that's all she wanted on this particular day, was to find a solution, even if it happened to come from him.

She ate part of her sandwich and he drank his sparkling water and a man wearing a brimmed hat at the other end of the bar complained. He had an English accent, "This is not a Greek Salad."

The Bartender tugged on his plate while offering, "Sir, I'll be happy to bring you something else from the menu."

But the Englishman held onto his plate, "I don't mind the salad, in fact, I quite like it, it's simply not

Greek, is the point I was trying to make."

The Bartender lowered his voice and spoke as elegantly as the Englishman, "If you want a Greek salad, perhaps you should go to Greece."

The Englishman insisted, "I happen to like the salad, although it's false advertising as the Greeks don't put arugula or any type of lettuce on their classic Greek salads. It's simply not done."

The Bartender then asked, "What do you want then?"

She and the Boss' Number One Assistant both laughed, albeit mildly. "What do you want," her Boss' Number One Assistant asked. "If you could have anything in the world, what would it be?"

She told him, "I can't have what I want."

"I have permission to give you the company credit card and you can go away for a week or so to regroup. Maybe go to a spa or something. You know, pamper yourself. You've been through a lot."

She told him, "No thank you."

"You want to go to Indiana?" he asked.

She was caught off guard and shook her head no. "What's in Indiana?"

She stopped eating. She was embarrassed, but answered all the same. "I don't know what's in Indiana, I'm just a little stumped by something someone I barely know told me about Aristotle, that's all. It's a crazy tangent. Nothing more."

"Look, whatever you are going through, whatever you are feeling, everybody wants to help but nobody knows how. Least of all me. Nobody except people in white lab coats or monks in brown robes knows how to deal with death. People at the office, they're...

uncomfortable."

She apologized.

"Don't you know, you are what everybody's scared of? You had it all and you lost it all."

"All?" she asked.

He looked at her for the first time, "All equals love, right?"

She almost brightened, "You could tell? You of all people? We don't know each other very well, do we? For example, I don't know anything about you."

"You've got to get over it," he told her, "Or pretend to get over it."

"I'm trying, I'm sincerely trying."

"Well, you're doing a bad job. Take some time off, take it as a gift. If you want to go get scrubbed at a spa, or go get some therapy, or go to acting school to learn to pretend you are better, or go upstate to be with nature, or go find out about a tangent in Indiana, or go find Socrates in Greece…"

She corrected him, "Aristotle."

"You want to go find Aristotle, go find him."

"He's dead", she said, referring to Aristotle, but he took it the other way.

"I can put Greece on the corporate card, but no more than a week."

She admitted to him, "My whole reason to find out some obscure information about Aristotle is more than likely a dead end. My lead might be a crazy person, or worse, as of today, might not exist at all."

"A dead end on a Greek Island, or two, cannot be a bad thing."

"No, if I went, I'd probably just go to Athens."

"So you've already thought about it," he says.

"I didn't realize I had."

"So then it's done."

Before she responded, he was already standing up and already paying the bill.

CHAPTER EIGHT

WHAT WAS SHE doing on a plane going to Greece, she asked herself. She knew how and why she got on the plane, but at the same time, she had no deep feeling that being on the plane was the right thing to do. Nor did she feel it was ultimately the healthy thing to do. But since she had come up with no alternative, in all of life's rich alternatives, she had chosen the wild card to Athens. But what was she really going to find? Would she discover knowledge that existed before Aristotle? Or, the truth about Aristotle? Did he ruin it for everyone? "It" meaning knowing. Or was he right and all the Thinkers that came before him were wrong? And how on earth or in heaven did she think she would be able to uncover the truth?

She looked forward to the more realistic day when thoughts of The Tourist and The Thinker would naturally be gone. That day was much more conceivable. Maybe by the end of this trip, The Tourist and The Thinker will have become part of the past. Her past.

Her flight couldn't have been more than a couple of hours in—she still had at least seven long hours ahead of her. She had already spent time consuming every single bite of the very bad airplane food. As distasteful as the packaged food was, she was grateful she hadn't had to worry about purchasing food beforehand. It had been one less travel-planning thing to worry about. Now she was faced with the fact that the movie selections weren't beckoning her to watch, nor was the canned music onboard beckoning her to listen. Moreover, she hadn't brought a thing to read and this was not by accident, this was by choice.

Her girlfriends had given her a half-dozen books for the trip. Mostly self-help books. Titles she couldn't remember. Most of the themes focused on Loss, including the famous Tibetan Book of Living and Dying. Another book given to her was meant to ignite her creativity. She left all these books behind except for the one filled with blank pages. The leather-bound black journal. Its empty pages were laced with silver trim. Her writer friend was encouraging her to write while she was away. All her artist friends, as they liked to call themselves—the photographers, the painters and the writers—had always wanted her to do something more creative. Be more creative. Be someone other than who she was.

Yes, she brought the blank journal, not to write a poem, not to draw or to sketch, not to write down her dreams, not to write a letter, not to write a book or a short story. She had brought the leather-bound blank journal to use as a notepad. She opened the leather book and turned its blank pages. She related to the empty pages because that's how she felt. Perhaps she wouldn't write any of her notes in it. Maybe she would simply carry the blank journal, with its silvery edges, as her silent companion. Two empty journals, side by side, on the streets of Athens. Her artist friends would have a field day with such thoughts.

It seemed to her that society gave more importance to art and artists than to non-artists trying to perfect the art of real living. Certainly she was grappling with real living, in fact she was failing at real living. But she had known about the art of being alive once, and it was greater than anything she had ever seen in a museum, greater than any scene in a movie, greater than any words on the pages of any book, greater than any notes from any instrument or voice; it had been greater than anything she had ever known or heard about. These thoughts reminded her why she was on the plane. It wasn't about The Tourist or The Thinker, it was about him. Because he was the one solitary person she had ever known who never wanted her to be anyone other than herself.

As embracing as he was of her, the truth was, she was not as embracing of him. And she knew that without having any distractions on this long plane ride ahead that she would be forced to think about the other side of Real Love. The other side of Real Love was the place where they weren't making unifying love, where they didn't agree, where she had wanted to run away.

As much as she had known she had Real Love and as much as she had known there were no betrayals between them, nor were there going to be betrayals between them in the future, the truth was she had at times tried to destroy love. Not every day but on random days. Even with the true facts of love right in front of her, there were moments when the dark thoughts came. The thoughts without any substance behind them. And her troubles, just like the physical make-up of womanhood, were strictly interior. An ordinary nuance of misunderstanding between them would, at times, unleash all the ugliness she kept hidden inside her, in the secret hiding place where she'd collected all the fear she'd ever known. All the anguish. When hopes turned into disappointments, she would place them there. When happiness turned into sadness, she added that to her collection. It was a lifelong work of experiences-gone-wrong, an emotional storage space that no one could see, therefore it did not exist. Until he, Real Love, came along to expose it.

Delusions of his wrong-doings would attack her and she would in turn attack him. Profanities were created for him, obscenities spoken to him. Air-borne objects came from her hands—not directed at him, but in front of him for his eyes to see. She wouldn't tell him she was leaving him; she would ask him to leave. "Please leave me. Please, you can't possibly want to be with this person," she would plead. "You deserve better," she would shout in rage.

In the aftermath of such behavior, she could barely keep her heart from sinking. What lower thing could anyone do than to decimate love, or try to? With all they had, the fact that she would declare war without an opponent was mystifying to her.

During her moments of viciousness and doubt, though, he never countered with a threat. He tried to reach her through words and through physical contact, but she was unreachable, as reaching towards an invisible hiding place is almost impossible. Reaching towards a woman without her permission is almost impossible. So he would instantly forgive while he waited it out. Hands-down, instant forgiveness. His capacity for exoneration and acceptance bewildered her and made her angrier. It was something she could not understand. While he could not understand, with all the love they had, how she could allow anything real or illusionary to come between them. Yet, he never left when she asked him to. He never returned her violence. He never broke a thing.

His limitations were different than hers. Just as tangible and masculine as his sexual composition. Whether his problems were valid or illusion, they were painful for him to experience and equally painful for her to witness. Whether his troubles were between them or outside of them, he never took them out on her. He might tremble or weep, he might rant, he might shout, but he never shouted at her. During his dark episodes, she would wait for the right moment, whether it took minutes or hours, in which she almost always knew instinctually how and where to place a gentle hand on him. And with this simple act he was willing to let her aid him, because he knew his external fears could be vanquished by virtue of being two rather than one. No matter how dismal life seemed to him at any particular time, he was open to her help. He welcomed any one of her methods whether it was spiritual love, silent love, intellectual love, puppy love or high voltage sex love. And during his darkest moments, he never once threatened to leave her side. And if he was ever tempted to, he never told her.

All these thoughts did not make her sad, though. They reminded her of her great fortune in knowing him. She had aspired to his kind of love, but never made it there. She gave him the best that she could. And strangely, miraculously, elatedly, that was enough for him.

She thought again about art and artists. How Michelangelo was said to have experienced great darkness while he painted The Sistine Chapel, or how Van Gogh's tragic life can be seen in his every brush stroke, or how Picasso's search for love, or groping for love, caused a new movement for painters in his era. And that without fighting through the darkness, none of their great works would have come into the light of day. She would never paint anything herself, but when she looked back at Real Love, she saw it as a work of art. All their love and belief, all their hope and joy, all their fear and darkness, and all their deep flaws had somehow fit together to become a perfect masterpiece.

And then she heard the sound of applause. Half the passengers were clapping and a couple of stewardesses were as well. The plane had just touched to the ground. It was a tradition, she heard someone in the row behind her say; Greeks and other Mediterraneans applaud whenever their aircrafts land. She had arrived in a place she never before imagined she would go. She had not had the desire to go to Greece when her friends were taking those cheap trips to the islands, back in the days before the euro. She had heard stories from friends who took random boat rides from Athens to random islands, Patmos or Hydra, without knowing where they would be sleeping that night. Her friends would arrive at such islands and would walk until they found the right hotel, or right bed & breakfast inn, never worrying that they might never find a place to sleep because they always did. Once, she heard, they stumbled onto an entire house for rent, with multiple views of sunrises and sunsets, for pocket change. Another time, an old Greek woman rented them her spare room, hardly charging them at all. Her friends always found a place to sleep, which they would describe in detail. But it was not the details she remembered from their stories; she remembered how daring she thought it was to show up somewhere without a plan. And yet, here she was, just landed in a city she never thought about or desired to visit before. Yes, she had a hotel reservation somewhere in the Plaka, compliments of her Boss' Number One Assistant. Other than having a hotel reservation, she had no plan. Except for the abstract concept of fulfilling her deepest desire.

All women by nature desire to know.

And although her mind was reluctant to believe she was on the right track, her heart twinged, just a bit. A sensation she hadn't expected. Was it a ray of hope or a ray of insanity? Whatever it was, it was a very odd feeling inside. It was as if, for the most fleeting of moments, he, Real Love, were there.

CHAPTER NINE

SHE HADN'T LEFT her hotel room for an entire day. She did not blame it on jetlag; she took full responsibility for her apprehension of leaving the room. Instead of adventure on her first day in Athens, all she could do was to lie on the hotel room bed, watching the natural daylight travel the walls, ceiling and floor until the light faded away. It was completely dark for an unknown period of time until the streetlamps outside clicked on, gifting manmade light into her room. The artificial light never stirred. Every once in a while during the course of the day, she got up to look out her open window. She felt the warm air as it sometimes drifted inside, and the curtains of gauze barely swayed. The sun was much more powerful than she had expected—the white stone buildings were whiter because of the sun, and the blue sky was bluer for the same reason. It must have been the bluest sky she had ever seen. She also watched all the people below, paying closest attention to the locals—the older women in black with their strong, aged faces who mingled together, the aged men with leathery faces who also banded together. Their expressions seemed profound and also seemed to lack gaiety. There was also the more modern set—the beautiful women and men of the present calendar year, fashion-conscious apparel, some with loud colors as well as traces of traditional white and beige linen that must have been worn for centuries. The children who played in the streets didn't seem terribly different from all the other children she'd seen playing in any other streets. The Greek language filtered up and into her room, and as expected she could not understand a thing. To her, it was like watching a foreign film without subtitles; the untranslated words provided their own unique sound. Words in English were occasionally heard, whether from Americans, Britains or others. And occasionally she heard other languages that she couldn't place. The American voices seemed to sound the harshest. The tourists were easily identifiable and she knew once she stepped outside of her room, she also would become a tourist.

This time while standing at her window, long after nightfall, she was attracted to the far corner of the courtyard. The taverna that had been crowded all day was experiencing an evening lull. Maybe it was time, she thought. She could venture out now, at this very moment. Yet, she remained inside. Apprehension was not new to her. It's something she had lived with since she could remember living. The only bold thing she ever did was open her heart and give it to him. Otherwise, her life had been pretty steady, even-keeled as others might say, not rocky in the slightest.

The life of an accountant. And not a victim of such a profession; it was chosen. She had wanted to start her own accounting firm, but even that turned out to be too daring for her and so she ended up in a steady corporate job. She never claimed to have much of an imagination and never really wanted to venture beyond her comfort zone. It wasn't surprising to her that she had harbored herself inside the Greek hotel room and she was, no other way to put it, afraid to leave. She wasn't afraid of being harmed or attacked or getting lost. She wasn't afraid of her valuables being stolen, as she had nothing of value to steal. The only fear she had was that of mere exploration. Bizarrely she had come all this way to stand at her hotel room window, nothing but a faux explorer. What a waste of time and money. There were truly adventurous human beings who would have seen half of Athens by now. Yes, she desired to know, to truly know what she had come there for, but how do you voyage when you're not a born voyager? She didn't need to remind herself that she had done nothing outside the norm in life other than to find love. Hardly an accomplishment to anybody but him and her. He and she. The thought of him sent vibrations, of every variety, straight to the center of her heart. A momentary sense of heat or burning pierced inside her. Real Love.

She decided not to do the breathing exercises again as she didn't want to use such a gimmick on her emotions. She wanted to be normal enough to embody normal courage. Not big courage, but everyday, ho-hum courage. All she wanted to do was to get dressed and walk outside her hotel room and go get something to eat. Not a particularly bold move by anyone's measure. All she wanted in this moment, she told herself while immovable at her hotel window, was to leave her room, if just for a while. And then tomorrow, she would find another way out of her room. But tonight, all she wanted was enough fundamental, ordinary courage to go outside. And then inexplicably without further thought, she dressed herself, picked up her empty journal, opened the hotel room door and closed it behind her.

CHAPTER TEN

FEAR IS SUCH a waste of time she thought while sitting in the back of a moving taxi, more or less afraid of not finding what she had come for. But now she was closer than she ever imagined she would be. Yesterday she had become a tourist, and today she was still a tourist. For the first time, she felt an affinity with The Tourist who had told her about The Thinker. She wondered if The Tourist ever imagined that the woman who lost her wallet would be in a taxi heading towards Aristotle's Lyceum that he built back in 335 BC. In the sketchy research she had done, she had come across an obscure article that was at least a decade old. According to what she read, a few years ago when the Greeks were breaking ground for their new Museum of Modern Art, they rediscovered the original foundation of Aristotle's Think Tank, as the journalist called it. The Lyceum was at one time a gymnasium, a place for lectures and intellectual exchange, and was also where Aristotle kept his accumulated specimens. This was where The Thinker was to have lived and breathed philosophy for twenty years before vanishing for fear of his life. He fled, not wanting to be tried and convicted for free thought the way Socrates had been because, as she read, Socrates was executed by poisonous hemlock! It amazed her to think that in spite of herself, on looking for clues to Aristotle, she was learning about things she hadn't thought about learning before.

She figured that Aristotle's Lyceum must be the best place to start. By now, the Greeks must have discovered much more than the foundation. She had never been near an archeological excavation before. So if all went wrong, at least she could say she had been adventurous enough once in her life and could say to her friends, "I've been to Greece and I've seen Aristotle's excavations."

She laughed quietly to herself and then wondered or worried, what if she'd completely made up the whole thing about The Tourist in her head, the way crazy people do. Even though she wasn't imaginative, maybe she had imagined The Tourist. And so rather than having met a crazy tourist in New York, she had become the crazy tourist in Athens. Crazy and delusional.

The Taxi Driver then stopped and started speaking to a middle-aged man on the street who then got in the taxi and sat next to her. She asked them in English, what was going on, but they didn't answer. The taxi moved forward again. Some roads were bumpy, others were not and the noise of the city was at a high level. Massive drillings in roads, too much traffic, blaring car radios, buses and fumes. Maybe the chaos was no different than in New York City, but she felt that the chaos was entirely different if only because of the blazing sun and heat and concrete structures everywhere. The heat was suffocating and yet, strangely the heat gave her an odd feeling of strength. She clutched onto the internet printout she had brought indicating where the excavations were to be, and then she waved it at the Taxi Driver, asking, "Are we east of downtown Athens yet? Are we close to Rigillis Street?"

The Taxi Driver, without words, seemed to indicate yes. But she was unsure, the Middle-Aged Man in the backseat next her also indicated, without words, yes. And then the Taxi Driver stopped again to talk to another person on the street. This time, it was a Young-Vibrant Woman talking on her cell phone. The negotiation of sorts took a bit longer and then the woman also got into the back of the taxi while talking nonstop on her phone. The three of them squeezed together on the backseat. The Middle-Aged Man and the Young-Vibrant Woman inadvertently pushed her against the passenger door, her head pressed against the dirty windows—filthy and smudged. She tried to roll the window down but it was broken. She wondered why a taxi driver would keep his car in such a disgusting condition. Taxi drivers had more courage than accountants, she thought. Why wouldn't he wash his windows? She could hardly see much of Athens at this point because of the dirty window she was stuck against, and then the taxi stopped again. This time, he asked her for euros. She didn't completely understand, and so he wrote down the exact amount for her to pay, and so she paid him.

Before she got out of the taxi, she asked where the excavations were, as if he understood her. The Taxi Driver pointed her to an industrial area without any markings. It seemed okay, it seemed she was near a downtown vicinity like she was supposed to be. She thanked him, then got out of his taxi, walking in the direction he had pointed.

Before crossing the congested intersection, she noticed a small wooden box with a glass window bearing a cross. She knelt down to look more closely. Inside the box was a photo of a very young girl, blond, maybe seven years old. The girl must have died or been killed right where she was kneeling. She was not religious at all and yet as if it were the natural thing to do, she closed her eyes and sent the young girl a prayer. When she stood up, she reminded herself that everyone has lost someone or will lose someone in his or her lifetime. And that love of any kind, every kind, is irreplaceable. The Very Young Blond Girl, who she would never know, gave her the smallest ounce of bravery to move forward.

She crossed the intersection exactly where the Taxi Driver had told her. All she could see were ordinary buildings. Basic Greek architecture. Perhaps one was an office building. There were no signs or postings indicating Aristotle's Lyceum, Aristotle's University or Aristotle's excavations. She kept moving forward, seeing nothing, feeling nothing, until she came across a giant hole in the ground, cordoned off, without markings or fanfares. Whatever it was, whether it related to The Thinker or didn't relate to The Thinker, it was closed to the public. She moved towards the barricade and then trespassed beyond it. Rubble and more rubble, was all. A few workmen in the distance drilled deep into the ground. Was this Aristotle's rubble or someone else's rubble? What difference did it make really? One set of reflexes signaled her to burst into tears, while the other set of reflexes signaled to her the utter foolishness of expending such emotion. She could almost hear her Boss' Number One Assistant's voice, "A dead end on a Greek Island or two, cannot be a bad thing."

But she wasn't on an exotic Greek Island, she was in the center of the smoggy, exhausting city of Athens. Foolish and alone. And yet she kept moving forward, toward the workmen, hoping one of them might be able to help her. And then a Greek man in a business suit, wearing a hardhat, approached her. He spoke to her in English, succinct, "There are places for tourists and this isn't one of them. If you want to know about ancient Greece there are existing museums listed in your tour guide. Most people start with the Acropolis." He pointed her in the direction to leave, exactly where she had come from.

"Do you know anything about Aristotle that's not mentioned in a tour book, that's not public knowledge?" she asked.

His only answer was a Mediterranean glare that landed deep into her eyes until she gave up and walked away.

After crossing back over the barrier and retracing her steps, she was back at the intersection where she started, standing beside the Young Blond Girl's small wooden box. She began to search for another taxi, when she noticed her first Taxi Driver was only a block ahead, stuck in traffic. The taxi had stopped to pick up another man and his backseat was full again. This time, the Middle-Aged Man was pressed against the dirty window. The taxi started moving again, but she ran towards it, as if there were a reason that his taxi was better than any other in Athens. She ran a few blocks trailing the taxi until she caught up with him. While running, she tapped on his window until he stopped. They negotiated. She spoke in English, he spoke in Greek. Neither one of them understood the other, except that she needed a ride and he could give her one. All this while the Young-Vibrant Woman in the backseat, in between the two male passengers, was still talking on her phone.

She climbed into the front passenger seat next to the Taxi Driver and then he navigated the taxi forward again. The Taxi Driver couldn't help but noticing that she was out of breath and shaking. He spoke in Greek, asking her if she wanted to go to the Acropolis, he pointed toward the site.

She told him no, and she told him everything in English as if he could understand. "I want to find anything I can about Aristotle because I want to know if I will ever see my Real Love again. I'd heard, as crazy as it sounds, that it's Aristotle's fault that I only believe I'll see him again rather than knowing I'll see him again. Because, I do believe it, but I want to know it." Then she took a breath and then she quoted her version of The Thinker's words, "All women by nature desire to know." She continued, "I know it seems nuts, but I need to do anything I can to find out more about Aristotle. I know I'm not a good researcher, I know I'm a terrible traveler and I know I've never been that interested in history, but I just want to know. Will I ever see him again? I need to know. And if it turns out that I'm crazy, I need to know that too."

The Taxi Driver avoided hitting another vehicle, or two, while listening to her. He did not understand her words, but he could understand that she needed something important.

The Young-Vibrant Woman in back had stopped talking on her cell phone and asked to look at the computer printout. The three passengers in the back read the page that was titled: Aristotle's University. The Young-Vibrant Woman then spoke, "Academe. Maybe go to Plato's Academe? Aristotle studied there, under Plato, maybe twenty years before going out on his own."

The three backseat passengers and the Taxi Driver argued in Greek as to where Plato's Academe was. The Young-Vibrant Woman tapped into her cell phone which, it turned out, was the market's latest Blackberry device. Shortly thereafter, she hand-wrote an address across the computer generated page.

The rest of the ride was quiet. No one spoke, the Young-Vibrant Woman did not make another phone call. Along many of the city roads she saw more wooden boxes with glass windows and crosses—more photos inside depicting loss of every kind. The Taxi Driver dropped the Young-Vibrant Woman off first, and then the other two men separately. He did not pick up any more passengers on the way as he drove to another area in the city, not remote in the slightest. Not long thereafter, the Taxi Driver moved through another busy intersection and then turned left onto a road that seemed to be forgotten. He slowed the vehicle down and with uncertainty pointed towards a run-down park with nothing in it but trees. He shrugged, then reexamined the handwriting of the Young-Vibrant Woman. They must be in the right place, mustn't they? And yet, nothing seemed to be there on the other side of the road. No signs, no plaques. Not even a wooden box. The Taxi Driver nodded her forward. She paid him more euros and started to get out of the vehicle, but stopped to give the Taxi Driver the smallest of embraces, a neighborly American hug. He accepted the inappropriate act though he did not return it. Unaffected by it, he nodded her towards the park again. She got out of his taxi, moved towards the most unremarkable park she had ever seen and did not look back.

CHAPTER ELEVEN

THE SPARSE TRAFFIC delayed her from crossing the moment she wanted to, but she did not have
to wait for a long stretch of time. She stood under the
scorching sun while a couple of agricultural trucks
rumbled by. She knew simply by looking across the
road there wasn't much for her to see when she noticed an old worn-out shoe in the middle of the intersection. Strangely, no vehicle had run over it, yet. She
wondered how a person could lose only one shoe. A
pair of shoes maybe, but one? Of course, she had seen
single abandoned shoes on their own before and wondered the same exact thing every time she had seen
one. Then the traffic opened, and all sounds of the 21st
Century evaporated.

As she walked across the silent road, on passing
the old shoe, she heard an audible voice. *"Whenever you
see one abandoned shoe on its own, it indicates that someone has left one world, and has entered another."*

She stared up at the burning sun, knowing she
had imagined the voice and when she replayed the
sound of the voice in her head, she couldn't detect or

remember whether the voice had been a man's voice or a woman's voice and yet the voice seemed as real as the road she was on.

When she reached the other side and arrived at the supposed university that Plato was to have created, she was worn out by sheer gratefulness that she reached a destination regardless of the result. She didn't expect much and yet she wanted everything. Not only was there nothing in the park, there was no one in the park. The lawn, if you could call it that, was uncut grass sloping upward along a stonewall that stood only two feet high. There were plenty of large broken stones, ancient and decayed, that were in the shape of blocks. There were other broken stones that were smaller and looked to be the most common of rocks. It might have been Plato's University once, but if she hadn't been guided there, she would have walked right past it on her way to some place else. From what she could see, there were no places to sit. She headed along the smallest of inclines past all the stones, towards a rundown staircase, observing hardly anything at all when an old man startled her.

The Old Man who spoke in Greek only, was barefoot and by looking at his feet had been without shoes for quite some time. His clothes were perhaps made of burlap, threadbare and faded brown. He introduced himself in Greek—speaking fast, he seemed to want to tell her something. She listened as if she could understand and then every once in a while in his ramblings, she could decipher an English word or phrase. In gregarious fashion, he gestured with his unwashed hands and arms while offering her a tour of the park—she did not let on she already knew there was nothing to see. He seemed to say he had been an attendant there for thirty years but she could not be sure. She assumed rightly or wrongly that he was a homeless man and that at the end of his private tour, he would ask her for money. She didn't expect that he would beg, as he seemed to be the most elegant homeless man she had come across.

And then, he took her hand. She knew she had been inappropriate when she had, without thinking it through, hugged her Taxi Driver. Now this Old Greek Man was more inappropriate than she had been. What's more, it seemed natural. She maintained her opinion that she wasn't afraid of being harmed, attacked, getting lost or robbed. And at the same time she maintained the opposite opinion that she had no courage. The combination of thoughts made no sense, and yet, to her, they were both true.

All the while, she let him hold onto her hand while pulling her along the rim of the Academe, as he called it. He talked fervently and sincerely and she didn't absorb one thing. He pointed to a ditch or hole in the ground. He talked about this for quite a while, he seemed to say that this was where Plato had planted an olive tree and that a tour bus had hit it and that the tree had been taken away. He seemed quite upset about the ordeal. On the other hand, he seemed quite pleased that at least the modern world had carbon-dated proof that the origin of Western Thought began where they were standing. And then he clarified the dates, according to him, the most crucial time of origin was a two hundred and eighty year period that began in 600 BC and ended in 320 BC. It fascinated her to think that she could derive such information, whether true or false, from a homeless man who was speaking in Greek. Was she imagining that she could understand him, or did she in fact, *under-stand*. Could one have a dialogue, an exchange with someone in another language, both languages completely foreign to the other, and somehow understand each other?

The Old Greek Man kept talking, or was it a lecture? Most of the things she did not understand. His 'guided tour' couldn't have taken more than a half hour because the park was so small, and had nothing in it. He led her to the center of the field, or campus as he called it, amongst all the stones. It was then he took both her hands. He looked directly into her eyes as if they had known each other their entire lives and then asked her in Greek, but, again, she heard his words in English.

"Why have you come here?" he asked.

Without hesitation, she told him, "To know."

He seemed emotional on hearing her response. A sense of happiness, if not relief, that someone had come searching for something, anything. He responded, "Then you must do everything to know, knowing you may never know."

"Will I ever see him again? I believe I will, but I don't know. I want to know. I need to know."

"There is only one good: knowledge. And one evil: ignorance."

She asked him the same question again. The same thing she asked everyone, every time.

He chose not to answer any more of her questions. Instead, he pointed towards the ground, towards the stones. "Permit me to suggest—you need to sleep."

She looked around, and questioned him, "Here?"

He continued pointing towards the stones. "Permit me to suggest—you need to dream."

"I need more than a dream, I need the truth."

"Permit me to lead you to knowing?" He asked.

She conceded with a nod between them.

"You are carrying exhaustion."

She was embarrassed. "How can you tell?"

He pointed at the stones again. "You need to dream, you need to lie down."

She laughed nervously, "Now?"

He didn't laugh. "You must."

He got down on his knees and then moved to lie down atop the stones. One of the smaller stones, he used as if it were a pillow. While looking down at him, it did appear he was lying on, literally, a bed made of stones, but no one, not even The Ancient Thinkers would have slept on rocks, she imagined. He spoke again in Greek, this time she didn't understand. He stood up again and then suggested that she try it.

Then somehow, without being afraid and without courage, she got down on her knees and moved to lie down on the stones. It was uncomfortable. He gazed down at her, warmly. On returning his gaze, she realized he hadn't asked her for any money.

Surrealism soon became her anchor as she started to feel better than she had felt for a long time. Her measure of time being, since she lost Real Love. The feeling of becoming lighter, the feeling of becoming gentler. There was a heat wave above and yet the stones were cool and a mild breeze found its way onto her skin. It was as if The Old Greek Man were a doctor. In the way she used to trust all doctors as a young girl—those days of her youth when she'd go to any doctor's office believing all doctors knew more than she knew. The Old Greek Man was some kind of doctor. Not a medical doctor, perhaps a doctor of the mind, or a doctor of the soul. He, whether a homeless man or a doctor, was not going to tell her the answer she wanted. The Old Greek Man, in his own peculiar way, was telling her to find the answer herself.

She was calm for the first time in her measurement of time, growing tired without becoming drowsy, without becoming sleepy. The Old Greek Man told her one last thing before she fell, "The world you are going to only makes sense when you are embedded in it."

And then, in that ideal instant, she fell into the deepest of sleeps. Slumbering, floating. Innately peaceful. Moreover, hopeful.

CHAPTER TWELVE

ALL THE NOTES made perfect sense. The sound of stringed instruments played in her head. The sound of a crowd of people murmured in her background—their words were incomprehensible. If there were dream images, there were none she could see. It would have been pure rest if it weren't for the fly buzzing around her. At first, she kept her eyes closed, while swatting the flying insect away. Annoyingly, the fly kept returning, usually at a faster speed, the way flies do. And so when she opened her eyes to get rid of the fly, she could hear the stringed instruments continuing to play and voices in the background continuing to murmur. Another man was standing over her, frowning. This was clearly not The Old Greek Man. She sat up, swatting the fly, but the man grabbed her arm, stern. He told her, "Flies should never be harmed. They're sacred."

She pulled her arm back, not afraid of being hurt, she simply wanted her arm back. "Since when were flies sacred?" she asked.

"They always have been," he answered matter-of-factly.

"According to who?"

"Whom," was his only answer and then he extended a very strong handshake, helping her up. A giant smile replaced his frown and then he insisted, "Please, call me Friend and I will call you the same, Friend."

He had a full head of white hair and yet couldn't have been more than the age of thirty. He was exceptionally thin and wore a clean, layered white linen suit, thick tan leather boots and had several golden rings on both hands, with gems she had never seen before. His eyes sparkled the same color his gems sparkled, in blues and greens.

There must have been hundreds of people in the park now. It was beyond overwhelming, contemplating how they all arrived without her hearing them arrive. She couldn't have slept that long, if at all. It made absolutely no sense. She looked around for The Old Greek Man, but she didn't see him anywhere. She asked her new 'Friend' where The Old Greek Man was, but he did not seem to know who she was talking about. Instead, he pulled her through the throng. The collection of people did not appear to be a collection of strangers as there was a high level of camaraderie, and excitement. He asked, "Do you like music?"

She answered, "Doesn't everybody?"

Her New Friend pulled her up the grassy incline towards the staircase. Everybody seemed to know him and he seemed to know everybody. There were women and men alike, all getting along. Her New Friend pulled her up the stairs and once they reached the top, the park became a kind of campsite with an open-air music hall in the center where many people played unfamiliar stringed instruments. Larger than violins, and smaller than cellos, the string instruments resembled miniature harps that were being played or strummed, as a guitar would be, all the while emitting classical overtures. After asking what the stringed instruments were, her New Friend answered proudly, "They're my Lyres."

She'd heard of lyres before but she had never seen one, not even a picture of one. She noted how refined and delicate they were.

To clarify, this was not a concert. This was a group of ordinary people, dressed not so ordinarily scattered across the campsite, simply playing music. Some players were in sync with other players, while many others were not. The sound and the idea of ordinary people playing music together lulled her, because music was never ordinary. And above all, they were all playing Lyres.

Her New Friend pulled her through the most mismatched group of people she had ever seen in one place. A stranger collection than the whole of the New York she knew, although the Athenians might find New Yorkers stranger than Athenians. Some wore denim jeans and t-shirts, while others wore three-piece suits or tuxedos. Some women and men wore gowns; one woman wore what looked like a tennis outfit reminiscent of the Billy Jean King era. Whatever anyone had chosen to wear, they seemed completely comfortable. Then she noticed other groups of women and men in white old-fashioned robes. She wasn't sure if the robes were religious attire, maybe they were priests, nuns, or maybe they were actors. Or maybe based on this unconventional gathering, the religious attire could have been their most favorite or most comfortable thing to wear having nothing to do with belief. In any case, she had never been in such a hospitable atmosphere before with so many people she didn't know.

Before she realized it, her New Friend had let go of her hand. Exactly at that time, a White-Robed Woman emerged, offering a plate of food and a glass of wine. But she instinctively declined.

The White-Robed Woman insisted with great kindness, "You need to be fortified to complete your travels."

"How do you know I've traveled, is it that obvious I'm a tourist?"

"Everyone travels to get here. Some people travel for days, weeks, just to ask their question."

"What question is that?"

"Well they're all intrinsically personal, don't you think? Every one has one unique question they are deeply longing to have answered, even if it is the exact same question."

"That makes no sense."

"Most people, at least once in each lifetime, are plagued by one burning question and they can't move forward until they manifest their answer. Isn't that why you're here?"

"Do you have one burning question?"

The White-Robed Woman smiled, "Not anymore."

"And that's what everybody's doing here?"

"Some people have questions, others of us are facilitators. We are here to help each individual find their answer."

"Okay. So, how do I get my answer?"

The White-Robed Woman's focus moved to another newcomer who was standing at the top of the staircase alone. This was a Male Teenager with a backpack almost as tall and wide as the boy himself. He seemed frightened. She watched the White-Robed Woman gracefully make her way through the campsite towards the frightened Male Teenager.

By all accounts, it seemed the White-Robed Woman had just abandoned her in the way the man in the white linen suit, her alleged New Friend, had abandoned her. Both of them had somehow vanished from sight. She wondered if she would ever see them again. Not that it made much difference. She also wondered if she would ever see The Old Man in the Park again. She turned to face the western edge of the site, when she saw the man in the linen suit, her New Friend, standing in the center of a circle surrounded by a crowd of avid listeners. She moved towards the western edge and by the time she reached the circle, her New Friend had vanished again.

The environment as friendly as it was, intimidated her. It felt as if she might have stumbled into the epicenter of a private club or a religion. She had never been interested in exclusivity of any kind. Or was it worse than that? Had she found herself in the middle of a cult? Or was this a gathering of theatre or movie industry people?

She then looked towards the eastern edge of the site where, for only what seemed like a split second later, she saw her New Friend again. This time, he was withdrawing behind a linen curtain, the same shade of white he was wearing. An older woman draped in black sat in the only chair on the scene—she seemed to be guarding the entrance to the curtain. She couldn't help but gravitate toward the eastern edge, where she approached the Woman in the Chair. She asked the Woman where her New Friend had gone to, but the Woman simply shook her head, no. She asked if she could go past the curtain to look for her New Friend. All the Woman in the Chair would do was to shake her head again. No. Many others approached the Woman in the Chair. Each received the same non-verbal response from her. The stream of quest-makers went on and on. Many chose to sit down on the ground outside the curtain and wait. She watched as each and every quest-maker was getting the same rejection she had received. Not one rejected quest-maker seemed to react negatively as they all believed they would eventually get to speak to the man in the linen suit.

She overheard a few of the quest-makers talking about her New Friend: "He is the most brilliant man alive."

"He is a sky-man."

"He is a bi-locator."

"He told me to call him Friend."

"The Old Guard Woman in the Chair overly protects him—for she is his mother!"

The sun had begun to set and most everyone's eyes had moved towards the brilliant orange flame going down for the night. The clearest alignment of stars replaced the sun; the stars shone down onto the grounds followed by the fullest of moonrises. There was no need for alternative light while the symphony of lyres continued to play into the night.

While the star and moon gazers gave their rapt

attention to the heavens, she decided to do something she wouldn't ordinarily do. In fact, she hated people who skipped or cut in lines—whether at ballparks or grocery stores or at the movies. The word hate was too strong, but the emotion of hate would come up anytime someone elbowed himself or herself in front of any line. She knew she didn't have much time to lose and so she decided to empathize and forgive all those who had committed the crime of cutting in front of her in any line and hoped all those at the campsite who might witness her petty crime would forgive her. All quest-makers and facilitators were transfixed by the cosmos, including the old Woman in the Chair, her New Friend's Mother, who was guarding the curtain.

She heard her New Friend's Mother chanting to herself. "All is one, all is one." It was during the Mother's chant that she took the opportunity to slip behind the linen curtain where she found nothing but earth and trees and the exact same all-is-one cosmos. She tiptoed across the ground as if there were any one else there, and called out the only name she thought to call him. "Friend, are you back here?" "Friend...?"

She heard his voice, but did not see him. "You're not supposed to be back here," he said.

"I've come a long way and I was hoping for advance forgiveness."

"Everybody's traveled far to get here."

But she still couldn't see him. She asked, "Where are you?"

"Mere steps away. Down here."

She followed the sound of her New Friend's voice towards a hole in the ground where she discovered him lying down, wrapped in a red blanket that matched the red color of the earth.

"What are you doing down there?" she asked.

"If I tell you, do I have your word not to divulge my secret?"

"Of course."

He climbed out of the ground, brushing off the red clay first. After which, he unwound himself from the blanket, carefully, then folded his blanket neatly. His layered suit was still a crisp white. He looked rather malnourished, but she didn't mention it. He then told her, "Dream incubation."

"What's dream incubation?"

"When the Gods speak to us through our dreams."

"So you believe in the Gods?"

"I don't believe in them, I know them."

"Theoretically, I suppose."

"Personally," he answered.

It was the first time since she lost Real Love, she did not feel utterly lost. Everything up to this point that had made no sense before, the same everything suddenly had the smallest thread of logic to it.

"So then, are you the one I can ask my question to?"

"Is your question more urgent than anyone else's? Worth skipping in line for? Worth one-upping your fellow woman or fellow man for?" he queried.

"You are correct in that skipping ahead of others, for whatever reason is an unworthy act. My question is definitely not more urgent than anyone else's, although it *feels* more urgent. I don't understand it myself, but I can't seem to do anything until I know. I'm driven beyond my own comprehension of myself to know. *All women by nature desire to know, just as all men desire to know."*

"And so Friend, what can I do for you?" he asked.

"You wouldn't happen to know anything about Aristotle, would you?" And then she added, "Friend."

He looked at her blankly, specifically not answering her question.

"Do you know anything about Aristotle?" she asked again.

She stared at his blank look and he returned her gaze. She assumed, rightly or wrongly, that if he were supposed to be the most brilliant man alive and he didn't know who Aristotle was, he probably wouldn't admit it. More than likely, he would only acknowledge answers that he did know. She figured it wouldn't do either of them any good to force him to admit that he didn't know anything about Aristotle. Therefore, she did not persist.

The pair of them were both willing, mutually, to let the question go until he chose to break their silence with another question. "That is not your true question. Or, is it?"

He was right, that was not her true question.

"Whatever your truest question is, you're not meant to ask me, you're meant to personally hand over your question to a prophet."

"You're not a prophet?"

"Well, perhaps I am, but not one of those kinds of prophets, not of the spiritual nature. If I were a prophet, I would be a prophet of the mind. The Gods are the only ones who can answer your truest question. I can tell you how to procure your answer, but I cannot tell you your answer."

"Okay, I'm listening."

"You must be in harmony with music. "

"That's it?"

"Music is the key to everything."

He could see her reluctance. He offered his hand again and asked, "Will you trust me, Friend? For this brief time we have together, will you grant me your highest capacity of trust?"

She figured she had come this far, what did she have to lose? She could think of nothing. She took his hand, and he opened the curtain again. This time, he pulled her towards the northwest, towards a far away mountaintop she hadn't noticed before. He then said, "Repeat after me. For the Love of Wisdom, we shall go."

And she walked with more trust in heart than she could remember in her measurement of time. She repeated with every emotion she had stored up inside of her, "For the Love of Wisdom, we shall go."

She was not afraid of a thing nor did she grow tired or hungry as they walked through the entire nighttime, holding hands. They took the most remote, winding roads and rivers, always traveling at an upward incline. There were more wooden boxes, more images of loved ones encased in glass protected by crosses along the way. There was nothing romantic or sexual between her New Friend and herself other than the romance of his words, "Together, we are equal beings."

He enjoyed talking along the way and she enjoyed listening. He recounted eight of his past lives to her and whether she believed him or not, it didn't matter because she found his way of thinking and of speaking to be irresistible.

The majority of what he spoke about were things she had never heard about or thought about before. Had she lived before? She didn't really care. Would she live again? Now that was something she cared about because that could possibly relate to Real Love. And she knew Real Love was the only thing giving her the strength to keep going.

It was neither hot nor cold outside of Athens, it was the warmth of a childhood summer night. Nothing her New Friend spoke of ever gave her a clue as to where they were going and what they were going to do once they got there. Each step forward felt as if she were born to be there, on an open midnight road to somewhere else.

His verbal meanderings were precisely succinct and precisely unclear, "The interval between the earth and the sphere of the fixed stars is considered to be a diapason—the most perfect harmonic interval. The distance between the sphere of the earth to the sphere of the moon is one-tone. The sphere of the moon to that of Mercury is one-half-tone. Mercury to Venus is a half-tone. Venus to the sun is one-and-one-half tones. The sun to Mars is one tone. Mars to Jupiter is one-half-tone. Jupiter to Saturn is one-half tone. From Saturn to the fixed stars, one-half-tone. The sum of these intervals equals the six whole tones of the octave."

She knew nothing of what he meant or what he was saying, and yet it all seemed valid and true.

He stared up to the heavens often and it was before they reached their destination he looked up to the sky one last time, echoing what his mother had said, "All is one."

Her New Friend was clearly in love with the galaxy and simply by looking upward, she could understand why. As she looked skyward, she silently repeated the three words to herself.

It was just before the first ray of sunlight when they reached the northwestern mountain. When she asked where they were, he answered, "The edge of Greece."

Only then, did he let go of her hand.

CHAPTER THIRTEEN

A WHITE-ROBED Man greeted her. This time when her New Friend disappeared, she did not feel abandoned. The White-Robed Man had the contrasting traits of being exceedingly kind and exceedingly impersonal. He made her feel as comfortable as he could, while guiding her without words to the center of another campsite.

There were similarities to the previous campsite, however, this one was much more organized, and somber. There were more people, hundreds, waiting in never-ending lines and there was more music. Softer voices spoke and restrained music was played. There were a few Lyres, as well as traditional stringed instruments; fewer notes were being strung. The atmosphere had a distinct lack of her New Friend's frivolity.

The White-Robed Man placed her in one of several lines of people where she waited at least a half-day like everybody else. There were several other White-Robed Men who all looked very much the same and she had a hard time telling the difference between them. There were other individuals, Beige-Robed, who offered bread and water. This time, she accepted. She tried to ask the gentlemen who stood in line in front of her, what everybody was waiting for, but he didn't answer her. He seemed distracted with his own problems. When she started to ask the gentleman behind her the same question, what are we all waiting for, she noticed he too was overly distracted. She decided to trust her New Friend, although he was no longer there, because he must have brought her there for a reason.

It was long after sunset when she reached the front of the line. The cosmos above reflected on the river's waters below, magnifying the moon and starlight almost double what it had been the night before. She thought it was the brightest nighttime she had ever seen and was wishing one of her girlfriends were there to share it with her, when she heard a female voice, which spoke aloud the very thing she had thought to herself. "It's the brightest nighttime I've ever seen."

She turned around to trace the voice, but it was impossible to know which woman had said it. Everybody there must be feeling something similar, she thought. And then, all is one, she remembered.

The woman's voice spoke again, "There's a constant beauty and tumultuousness to the Acheron River. As much as the Acheron River changes, it's always fiercely beautiful."

It was the first indication of exactly where she was. The Acheron River. Although she did not know exactly where The Acheron River was on the map, she knew it was on the edge of northwestern Greece because that's where her New Friend had brought her.

Another White-Robed Man handed her a writing instrument, one she didn't recognize. It resembled an antique fountain pen, but instead of ink, it had a blunt blade at the tip. He then handed her a lead tablet. She asked him, "What am I supposed to do?"

He answered, "Inscribe your question onto the tablet."

"And then what?"

"We take your question to The Priestess who will then ask God for your answer."

"Where is The Priestess?"

He pointed far into the distance. In the direction of a large, overgrown tree, but she couldn't see more than that.

Even though her mind believed it was a ludicrous act to carve her question onto a lead tablet and then hand it over to a Priestess for her answer, another part of her wanted to do it. The writing instrument scratched as she wrote, or engraved, her truest question onto her personal lead tablet: *Will I ever see him again?*

The White-Robed Man waited patiently and did not look at her question when she handed it to him. With reverence, he placed her personal lead tablet inside a basket, along with the questions from those who came before her.

"Now what?"

"We take the questions to The Priestess and you will have your answer tomorrow."

"When do we go?" she asked.

"No. You wait here overnight. We, the attendants, take the questions to The Priestess and then we come back with your answers tomorrow."

"Please let me come."

"That is not how it's done."

"Please."

He was exceedingly gentle when he explained, "I'm sorry, it cannot be." He turned his attention to the next person in line.

Never fully ready to give up, she tugged on the sleeve of his white robe, while asking as gently as she could, "And if I follow you, will you try to stop me?"

He did not encourage her, "We are nonviolent people."

"I'm the same, I'm nonviolent. I promise not to make a fuss; I will just follow and listen. Please, I am asking you. If The Priestess asks me to leave, I will leave. Immediately. You have my word."

She could see his inner struggle stretching across his face and moving down the side of his neck. His monk-like disposition and his irritation towards her were at conflict. It was against his better instincts that he said, "No worldly possessions, just the clothes on your back."

She was still carrying her handbag, which contained her passport, cash in euros and dollars, credit cards, a key to her hotel room and the computer printout. If lost, all were replaceable. Not hassle-free, but replaceable. She agreed.

And then she asked, "May I carry my own question to The Priestess?"

Before he could answer, she had already taken her personal lead tablet out of his basket.

"Thank you," she said again and again.

He pointed northwest and told her, "Meet me over there at the Divide in one hour."

There was nothing she could see indicating a Divide except wide-open terrain.

Before she could ask him, he answered, "You'll

know when you reach the Divide, as it is precisely where the wind picks up. You will not speak, you will follow. You have an hour to change your mind, and I humbly ask that you change it."

"Thank you," she repeated.

She reached the Divide early and waited alone. She looked down the slope and again, all she could see was a humungous tree and nothing else. When the White-Robed Man arrived, he was with other White-Robed Men, and all carried baskets filled with lead tablets. Each of them took his shoes off and her White-Robed Guide told her to do the same. He added, "We are at one with the earth when we abandon our shoes."

She took off her shoes and left her bag of worldly possessions behind.

Without being afraid and without courage, she then followed barefoot at the back of a single file line of White-Robed Men carrying baskets of other people's questions. She held her own personal lead tablet close to her heart and breathed in the open terrain and the wild reflecting river and the shining cosmos.

The constant breeze at the bottom of the hill was the only thing she could hear, since no one chose to speak. The breeze had a rhythm of its own, frenetic at times and lullaby-esque moments later. It was as her New Friend had told her, "Music is the key to everything. You must be in harmony with music." She had never thought of the sound of wind as music before, but now she couldn't imagine wind not sounding melodic.

And then she saw a Priestess appear under the large tree. The petite frame of the White-Robed Priestess emphasized the magnitude of the tree. The

Priestess was clothed in the same fabric the men wore, although her garment was wrapped more tightly, accentuating her feminine diversity. The same cloth was wrapped around her head that struck not of religion, but of royalty—a crown without diamonds.

The Priestess saw that the White-Robed Men had arrived and nodded towards them, acknowledging, it was time. The White-Robed Men carried the baskets of questions to her, setting them down at her bare, unwashed feet. When the Men walked away, she saw that The Priestess had noticed her for the first time.

She was nervous, standing there, waiting for The Priestess to react or to say something. When she received no reaction, she decided she had better place her burning question at The Priestess' bare feet as the men had done, and so when she went to set her question down on the ground, The Priestess reached down and took the lead tablet directly from her hand. The Priestess then silently read her question.

The Priestess' eyes bore into hers, and then she questioned her, "Do you know where you are?"

"Sort of, or I should say I know I'm on the edge of Greece, northwest, and that's the Acheron River over there and that you, personally, have a direct connection to God or to The Gods. "

"And do you believe in why you're here?"

"I wouldn't be here if I didn't."

"You are, we are, standing at the foot of the Oracle of Dodona. Where God speaks directly to us through the wind and the sound of the leaves as they rustle from this ordained Oak Tree."

"Do I have your permission to stay?"

"I do not have the power to send you away. If you

have crossed the Divide on your own free will, then God will certainly give you the answer that you need."

She was relieved—The Priestess was much more down-to-earth than her White-Robed Guide had indicated she would be. She wondered if they might become friends one day. But that's not why she was there, she was there to find out the answer to her truest question. *Will I ever see him again,* her heart sang. Strange she thought. Her heart used to say the question, and now her heart was singing it. She must be closer. Closer than she'd ever been. Already, she felt blessed in a way she had never felt before. And already, she felt closer to him than she could remember, in her measurement of remembering time. She felt for sure, she was close to Real Love. And it felt real.

Together, she and The Priestess, waited for sunrise. Silent hours passed by without words.

Before any indication of morning, she watched The Priestess instinctively place her knees on the ground. She did not know whether The Priestess was praying or meditating, as she had never known what the difference was. Even so, she tried to respect what The Priestess was doing by kneeling down to the earth, in emulation.

The Priestess watched and then instructed her, "All one need do is to thank The Gods for all that you have been given. Everything. Including all things you consider to be good and all the things you consider to be not good."

She took in what The Priestess had said, and then posed, "Everything but problems, right?"

"The sum of everything is a gift from the sky."

"Even a crisis?" she queried.

"Crisis is a moment of truth." The Priestess could see her dis-belief. "Once you have offered your sincere gratefulness, we can begin."

"May I at least ask, why should I be thankful for my problems?"

"No one can advance without them. Victories are easy. Triumphs bring about wealth, friends, notoriety. Solving our most difficult problems is the mastery of life. It is how we handle our deepest problems that defines our existence."

She hadn't traveled this far for a sermon and found it somewhat irritating at the time of her truest need with the most important question of her life carved onto a lead tablet. On the other hand, what did she expect? The woman after all was a Priestess, it must be part of her job. She felt conflicted and of course The Priestess could sense this.

The sun had already risen when The Priestess urged her on. "If you wait any longer, we will lose our opportunity. You must do what I say, to achieve your answer."

She didn't wish to argue with The Priestess, so she got down on her knees and tried her best to thank The Gods. Which Gods she was praying to, she didn't really know. They hadn't covered that, but she wasn't going to bring that up now. She was going to pray to whatever God or Gods were listening, in order to get her answer. She started with the easy parts first. Thanking the Gods for her life and for meeting her Real Love even though Real Love had been taken away. She was thankful for her family, for shelter, for her job, for her friends, for New York in general, for her life over there and then she began to be thankful for her Taxi Driver, for The Old Greek Man, for Her New Friend, for the Robed Women and Robed Men and for The Priestess. She really wasn't up for thanking The Gods for her problems, but she tried. She started with thanking The Gods for her job being in jeopardy because it made her appreciate her job more. She then thanked The Gods, although she wasn't sure she meant it, for other things she was unhappy with including the fact that her rent was being increased, and for the invasive insurance company that made her fill out a series of claim forms when she lost her Real Love. She finished her thankfulness list and knew very well she hadn't acknowledged the most important problem on her list.

Her biggest problem, moreover her only problem, was that she had lost Real Love. How or why could she thank anyone or anything for that, including God or The Gods? To herself, she said, "Thank you for taking away the love of my life."

But she didn't mean it. She tried again, "Thank you for giving me the love of my life, and thank you for the two years that I had with him."

She tried again, "They were the best two years of my life."

She then complained skyward, "Why since those were the best two years of my life, why would he be taken from me?"

She knew the Priestess wouldn't approve. She then thanked The Gods, "Thank you for taking the love of my life, Real Love, away." But she didn't mean it.

The Priestess knelt down next to her. "Maybe try, something like this: Thank you for giving me the gift of Real Love for two years. Thank you for taking care of my Real Love now. Thank you for my most difficult problem that I do not understand. The problem of losing Real Love. Thank you for leading me past it. Thank you for my life. Here and now."

She closed her eyes and tried to repeat in her mind what The Priestess had told her. It was difficult but she did the best she could do, knowing her thankfulness was far from complete.

She then stood up and asked The Priestess, "What religion is this? I don't know if I believe in it."

The Priestess did not look at her when she responded, "You should focus on what you believe in, and I will do the same."

And then The Priestess picked up two baskets, and asked her to do the same. They carried the baskets and placed them at the base of the Oak Tree. After moving all the baskets to the base of the tree, The Priestess instructed her to sit on whatever side of the Oak Tree she desired.

She chose facing west while The Priestess chose to sit on the opposite side of the tree trunk, facing east.

She watched The Priestess take the first question out of the first basket and then The Priestess whispered the first question aloud. She could not hear The Priestess' voice, and assumed that was intentional on The Priestess' part. Most of the burning questions must have been as highly personal as her question was. She appreciated The Priestess' discretion as the wind picked up, blowing the oak leaves above. The leaves shimmered and danced and created a consistent shade for them below. She did not hear a voice, but The Priestess must have heard something because she carved an inscription onto the back of the first lead tablet.

The Priestess picked up the second lead tablet and asked another silent question.

She knew it was time to ask her own question. Her own true burning question. She turned all her attention, past, present and future—every cell of her body, every feeling or memory she'd ever had or every feeling or memory she was yet to have—to this perfect opportunity under the ordained Oak Tree. She listened to the music that the wind and the leaves were playing. An endless rustling. She looked up and saw white doves circling just above the tree and below the sky.

True, it felt like God if there were a God. It felt like he, or she, or they, were there. If there were a God or Gods, it would feel like this. Powerful and reassuring. Pure and musical.

And she could also feel Real Love as if he were there. She could not see him, but she could feel him. His presence. As if he were lying next to her in bed, taking a walk with her, making her laugh, making love to her, greeting her hello or saying goodbye. She could, with all sincerity, feel him and believed if she were ever going to get an answer, now would be the time.

She held her question upward, facing it towards the heavens, and asked quietly, "Will I ever see him again?"

The rustling of the oak leaves picked up, and the branches of the tree parted, the bright sun shone down onto her lead tablet and then reflected back up into the sky, the oak leaves quickly closed again. And yet, she couldn't hear a voice.

She asked the question again, and she asked it more forcefully, "Will I ever see him again?"

There was no excessive rustling of branches or

leaves. Only a continuous wind and a mild shimmering of the entire Oak Tree. And no voice, not even an imagined one.

And on the third asking of her most burning question, it was the quietest, most peaceful rejection she had ever experienced.

She stopped asking the question but just waited, looking skyward until the moment came when she knew. She knew she was not going to get her answer here. There were no words for her up in the Oak Tree, there were merely oak branches and leaves swaying in the wind.

Upon her knowing that she would not know, she let out a guttural cry. Her cries echoed throughout the land. She assumed others could hear her sobs, but she could not help herself. She sobbed and wailed, draining herself of all emotion good and bad. She did not dry her tears; it was the breeze that dried them for her. When the tears stopped and the breeze stopped, she looked over to The Priestess, who was gone. The baskets of questions were gone. And the White-Robed Men were nowhere to be seen. Two black doves came out of nowhere, flew across the sky and then disappeared again.

She stood up and looked as far as she could see. Miles and miles of wilderness surrounded her. Beautiful and wild. Barefoot and alone, without a worldly possession and without a map, she wondered where she was and how she got there.

CHAPTER FOURTEEN

SHE HEADED BACK to where she remembered the Great Divide might have been. The path seemed correct but the closer she got, she could see that she was headed in the wrong direction. She tried other wrong directions until the only thing she could be sure of was right in front of her. The Acheron River. Without her New Friend and without any friend, she would follow the winding river backwards. Her chief concern was to remember which fork in the dozens of roads she should take to get to Athens. She hoped she would make it back to the Greek City before night-time, and she hoped she would pace herself so that she wouldn't get too hungry or thirsty. The earth scorched under her bare feet, but strangely it didn't take terribly long to get used to. In fact she remembered preferring to travel this way as a young girl. She and her childhood buddies, girls and boys alike, would take off their shoes whenever the adults weren't watching. Playgrounds and playfields were always better without restrictive shoes even if every once in a while, a day ended in blisters.

As she walked, she tried to be thankful for getting lost in northwestern Greece like The Priestess would have told her to. It was challenging, but she tried. And then she thought, rather than deceiving herself into a false thankfulness, perhaps it would be better to focus on the things she was seeing. She assumed if she made it back safely, she would never see the things she was surrounded by ever again. And so, she focused on the ever-changing colors of the river, the sky, the ground, the rocks, the grass, the trees and shrubs, the flowers and the sunlight. Everything, every step was filled with change, a kaleidoscope of natural sites and smells in slow motion. As fate would have it, every single change that occurred was good. Violets became lavenders that became purples. Yellows became oranges and then reds. There was every shade of lush green as well as burnt greens from the heat. The river went from blues to turquoises to browns and blacks to the color of crystal. Savage at times and surprisingly gentle at other times. Everything, every moment was changing as she walked and yet it all seemed to stay the same. It didn't make sense, but what did make sense was that she had a fullness of breath that she hadn't quite experienced since being a childhood girl without shoes. Was it the fresh air or was it the sound of things? There was absolutely not one modern sound—only that of the Greek blossoms and leaves and branches and grass and wind and the sound of the river's constant stream. Even a tumultuous river had its moments of peace. The natural sound of water going exactly where it's supposed to go. Downward, following gravity as all the living things surrounding The

Acheron were doing. And when she heard the sound of one bird or a flock of birds in flight, it calmed her. Everything, in untouched Greece, was in perfect harmony except for herself. How could she become part of nature's perfect harmony, she wondered?

It was then she started to get thirsty. She continued walking, trying to shake off the mere idea of thirst. No one had told her whether the river's water was contaminated or not. Back home, back in the U.S., there were many places you couldn't drink the water that should be drinkable. She had seen no signs posted, but even if she had, she couldn't have read the signs in Greek. She walked to the river's edge and kneeled. Instinctively, she gave thanks to the river before drinking from it, as if it were the natural thing to do. And then she cupped her two hands together, dipped them into the stream and drank.

The temperature of the Acheron River was milder than she imagined it would be. She drank and splashed water onto her face, and then splashed larger amounts of water along her arms and her legs. She looked around to see if anyone was watching and then laughed aloud, reminding herself no one, but no one was there. She took her blouse off first, hesitated only a split-moment before taking everything else off. She saw a glimpse of herself in the river's reflection. She saw a woman's body. Not a girl anymore and not yet an old woman. Was she at the middle of her life, or near the end? She examined her body in the reflection. She saw all the imperfections she wished would go away. The constant movement of the water and waves danced below her, illustrating how imperfectly perfect she was. Her sensuality reflected in the ever-changing stream.

She very well remembered that the last time she swam in a river was the very last time Real Love existed. But she could not blame her loss on this Greek River or any other body of water, for that matter. Her quest had nothing to do with blame. Her quest had only to do with her *natural desire to know.* She took a deep breath and was not afraid when she dove in. The river's current was strong but she, too, was strong and perhaps had become much stronger than she realized. She swam against rapids with ease and then let the rapids carry her back to where she began. So exhilarated by her new ability, she swam against the currents several times, letting the river carry her back to safety again and again until she reached physical exhaustion. Eventually, she taught herself to float on top of the river without effort. She imagined herself a cloud resting atop the river's surface and while she did this she heard nothing but the intermittent sound of underwater below and heaven-on-earth above. Butterflies and other insects of every color, some with silver wings, were also floating alongside her, cloudlike, skimming the water.

Not in her wildest dreams could she have imagined she would be lost in Greece, swimming naked in a river she had never heard of before and that she could experience a hint of happiness or contentment. She thought about Real Love and wondered what he would think. Had he given her the courage to come this far without him? Was this God's or The Gods' answer to her, that she would never see him again, but she would have the courage to go on? That was not the answer she wanted, and yet in this moment, she felt at peace with every single thing that had ever happened to her. Even the loss of Real Love. Even if the river took her away to meet her own end, she would be at peace. She questioned if the river did actually take her away, would she then see him again? She was elated and tired at the same time. An anchor of strength now resided in her, one she hadn't known before coming this far. It was this precise strength that would take her to the next place, wherever that was. And then she heard a grating or a mechanical sound. An invasion, a jarring of sorts. Was it machinery, she wondered? It was the first modern sound she had heard since Athens. The sound was drawing nearer. Perhaps it was a kind of motor. It was familiar and was not the sound of an automobile or a bus. And then it became clear, it was the sound of a motorcycle coming closer and closer. She leapt out of the water to clothe herself, when the sound of the motorcycle came so close that it stopped right in front of her.

Halfway dressed, she looked up and towards the driver: an unshaven, sunglassed, frazzled-looking man was staring at her from his motorcycle seat.

She turned her back to him while he asked in an Italian accent, "Shall I look the other way?"

She answered yes, and yet he did not look the other way.

Not until she was fully dressed, did she turn around. She approached him, head-on, "Should I be afraid?"

His only answer was, "No." And then he asked, "Do you need a ride anywhere?"

Her only answer was, "No." And then she asked, "Where are you going?"

He told her he wasn't sure.

When he inquired as to where she was going, she told him, "Athens."

He then said that he was going to Athens too and that it was a free ride, one without strings.

She didn't need to look around the wilderness again to know she needed the ride. She stepped closer and then took off his sunglasses, when she asked him again, "Should I be afraid?"

She tried her best to analyze his dark eyes, trying to gage fear versus safety. She didn't feel afraid, and so when he answered no once more, she climbed onto the back of his motorcycle.

He took off in the direction of Athens and told her, "Hold on tight and lean into the direction of the curves. Most people lean against the curves, which is a fundamental mistake. Always lean into the curve, it will keep you safe."

She liked hearing the word safe.

He took a fast curve immediately and she didn't want to hold onto him and she didn't want to lean into any curve, but she knew she didn't have a choice. She held onto him as if they'd known each other before and she leaned into the curves as if she were an intricate part of the Greek road and they didn't speak for many winding miles. His speed was exhilarating in some respects. The wind and sun on her face without sunscreen were supposed to be bad for her skin and yet it felt wonderful. She had put her trust in a stranger or had she put trust in herself—both components to the equation felt liberating. She most definitely missed the experience of walking barefoot and moving slowly on her own, and the natural sound of the Greek wild. The sights and sounds now went by almost too quickly and the only sound she could hear was the buzzing, blaring sound of the motorcycle.

She knew she should be grateful, so she thanked God or The Gods for the deafening sound of the motor and for the smell of the gasoline fumes.

They didn't speak for the entire ride, or if he did speak, she never heard him. He seemed to know exactly where he was going. When she saw the first road marked for Athens, that was the direction that he took. As the sun started to leave for the day, she could see the city lights ahead and she reminded herself of what safety meant: To follow one's instincts no matter what.

He then took a turn to the right up a winding hill. It didn't seem to be an obvious turn, but he seemed to know what he was doing and where he was going. Perhaps this was a local's shortcut and then she reminded herself, he was not a local, he was an Italian. She held onto her trust as they reached the top of the hill where the city of Athens was clearly seen. From where they were, the city looked like an empire.

Gathered at the top of the hill was a smaller group of people, not more than twenty, surrounding a campfire. Whether everyone knew The Italian or not, they seemed to want to know him. Men and women alike were entirely friendly but not excessive in the way that her New Friend's gatherings were. This was low-key bohemian. Lots of denim and leather. One young woman wore a tie-dye dress. It appeared that The Italian was the object of everyone's desire. Everyone's but hers. Food and drink in abundance. The Italian handed her a glass of wine but she declined. She wasn't in the mood for alcohol. He argued that wine was not considered alcohol—it was the drink of The Gods. She decided to accept the glass of wine and drank it with genuine pleasure. He raised his glass to hers and said, "The world is round."

Others lifted their glasses, echoing, "The world is round."

She laughed and raised her glass, "And it always will be."

But no one laughed with her.

It became pitch dark outside with but three exceptions: The campfire light, the distant city light coming from Athens below and the light from the moon above. Another full moon. She pondered how a moon could be full every single night she had been in Greece. She was not worried about not getting back to Athens, because now that she could see it, she knew she could walk there if anything suddenly went wrong. After all, she had gained strength and trust on the road, she didn't expect to lose it now.

And then together, everyone observed the beginning of a full moon eclipse. They all listened to The Italian describe in detail how the entire moon was passing through the earth's umbral shadow. "The sun is behind the earth," he told them.

Some people didn't understand what he meant, therefore he continued. "The umbra is the shadow created by the light source. In this case, the moon is totally shielded from direct illumination by the sun, providing us with the understanding that the earth is a sphere."

She found it hard to relax with all the people talking about the moon. Hadn't they seen an eclipse before? Or looked through a telescope in school? True, the changing colors of the moon were to be treasured—a fiery red orange had begun to alight the sky.

She wished they all would be silent. Gazing at the moon should not be an exercise in brainpower, she thought. Moon-gazing ought to be private and insightful, if possible. She sat down on the ground, distant from the others and with them all the same. It was the first time she had become still in almost a twenty-four hour period. Her body was reacting, adjusting to lack of movement. Her legs were quivering, as was the rest of her, weak and shaky. She hadn't realized how worn-out she was. Her spirit had zero fatigue, but her body had not an ounce of vitality. Someone offered her a plate of food. Most of what appeared to be meat and vegetables was charred and unrecognizable. Without questioning the food she had been given, she ate everything on her plate in gratefulness.

While everyone continued to speak in fascination about the moon, her personal umbral shadow superseded any additional thoughts of the moon. She concentrated on her own fascination. Nothing was better than Real Love. Nothing. It worried her to think she might be near the end of her road in pursuit of him. Was God or The Gods commanding her to give up? To let him go? Would everything after Real Love only be a replacement or a pacifier? And what a pacifier the Greek wilderness had offered. She was truly thankful.

She spoke silently to God or The Gods when she told them quite forcefully, "I know you may wish me to stop my journey now. I can see Athens below and I can imagine myself back on the plane going home. I can see that path. But what I cannot see is the yes or the no of, will I see him again? Until I know one way or another, I will not stop. I am thankful for everything you have shown me and given me. But I do not know, and I don't believe you have given me, my answer. Real Love was the best thing you ever gave me or will give me, so please I ask you with all sincerity, please let me know one way or another: *Will I ever see him again?*

And then she noticed that everyone had become as quiet as she was. Their faces became covered in a soft red hue from the eclipse. They all, including her, were in awe as they looked skyward. The only thing that could be heard was the wind from the hilltop, the embers crackling in the fire, and the breath of everyone who was there. No one spoke and it seemed it was as her New Friend's Mother had said, "All is one." Even though she considered no one there to be a friend, she was glad she was with them. Deeply glad. And maybe, she thought, they were all asking the moon their own questions—equally as silent and equally as sacred.

The Italian then moved to sit next to her. He moved so close to her that his legs were touching hers. They had already been this close on his motorcycle, but this closeness held a different sensation.

She felt his warmth when he asked, "What do you think of the moon?"

The only response she could think to tell him was what her New Friend had told her, "The distance between the sphere of the earth to the sphere of the moon is one-tone."

He smiled as he quickly concluded, "So you're a Pythagorean."

She laughed, "Definitely not. I'm not even sure what that means."

"You've just quoted the words of the world's most renowned thinker and you don't know who he was?"

"You mean Aristotle?" she asked hopefully.

"Pythagoras!" he exclaimed. "Don't tell me you've never heard of Pythagoras?"

"Well I vaguely remember something about the Pythagorean theory from school. Was it in geometry? Which I can't remember and confess, I was never good at."

He reached for a twig on the ground, laden with tiny white blossoms along its branch. With this, he drew a triangle onto the earth, as he explained, "The theorem states that in a right-angled triangle the square of the hypotenuse, the opposite side of the right angle, is equal to the sum of the squares of the other two sides."

"Oh, I vaguely do remember. It was a long time ago when I studied that. A lifetime ago. But what good does that do you, or me, now?"

"Well it means that all questions have answers is what it means."

"All questions?" she asked.

"All. Think of a question; you don't have to tell me what it is. Just contemplate deeply whatever it is you want to know. And once you've asked the question in silence and in completeness, let me know."

She closed her eyes and asked her most sincere question to the universe. Silently. When she opened her eyes, she felt his gaze.

His answer to her was this, "If the premise is true, the conclusion must be true."

She returned his gaze, taking in what he said. She repeated it aloud, for confirmation. "If the premise is true, then the conclusion must be true?"

"That is correct."

She reached her arms around him and held onto

him and he held her back. She could feel the others watching but she did not have the capacity to concern herself with other people's perceptions. This Italian was giving her permission, encouraging her, to keep moving forward. She knew she didn't need his validation but because he had given it to her so freely and so sincerely, it was precisely the only thing she needed.

She pulled her arms back, asking another question. "So is that true for every question?"

"Every sincere question. That's why I asked that you consider the question deeply. Many people roam around the earth asking questions when the answers they are looking for have no meaning. If you have a true question, then you have everything you need."

She thought about it. "You mean an empty question has no value?"

"Exact."

She sighed. "Where have you been for the last few months of my life, when I needed you?"

"I've been right here, where I always am."

"And where have I been?"

"You've never moved in your whole life. Haven't you always been where you are?"

She knew better than to question this. He was talking about bigger things—their spiritual lives and not their physical lives. She thought about Real Love and realized she had felt the same before Real Love, after Real Love left and during Real love. It was all the same, as Real Love had been with her the entire time. The time leading up to finding Real Love, for she had always felt him on the horizon. And after Real Love had gone, the feelings remained. And the glory of the present during Real Love. She hadn't considered this before and could hardly find a word to express this sentiment.

They sat silently together. He handed her the blossomed twig and she held onto it. He then placed his arms around her, again. He kissed the side of her face, more than once, and then he asked, "Do you wish to go to bed now?"

"I'm sorry. I'm not ready to go that far with another man. It's too soon."

He continued to hold onto her when he gently interrupted her line of reasoning, "And miss the highest form of divinity?"

"I agree that sex with love is the most divine exchange that can happen between two people, but we don't yet know each other. You very well may have saved my life, but we haven't reached that level and may not ever."

The Italian's smile became more and more handsome. "Sex. Not sexing together, not sleeping together. Dreaming together, alas. Dreaming is the highest form of divination. The highest, most ultimate link to The Gods."

She hadn't thought of herself as a typical American before, but it was the American female in her that had to outline the conditions, "You mean, dreaming together in the same bed?"

"Worry not, you would have your very own bed if you like. You can have more than one bed if you like."

He stood up and extended his hand down to hers. She allowed him to lift her from the ground. They held onto each other as they walked away from the group, and she held the blossomed twig close to her heart. She could feel other people judging her, but she didn't mind. Because she knew, even if no one else knew, her journey was real. Moreover, her question was sincere and she would go as far as she could go to find her true answer.

CHAPTER FIFTEEN

THE ITALIAN HELD onto her under the moonlight as they walked together down the other side of the hill—where the wilderness seemed wilder than before. They stepped in sync through barely walked paths, and they saw the blinking eyes of night creatures watching them as they went. The Italian spoke of the art of dreaming and while he did so she remembered that The Old Man in the Park and her New Friend also seemed obsessed with dreaming. The more he spoke, the more impassioned he became. He began to jump from one subject to another, ramblings on deduction and logic and truth and then back to dreaming. He asked her intermittent questions, always wanting, needing her feedback on every single idea he had. She kept up with him and answered as honestly and as best she could. The concepts that concerned him the most, including that of nonsense, were of little importance to her. These were intellectual excursions. Whatever he said whether true or untrue didn't carry that much significance to her, because what he had was the sincerity of truth-seeking. His deep caring for wisdom was what inspired her toward him. It was what kept her trust in him alive.

At one point he stopped walking and asked, "Do you know that some things are the case no matter what anybody may say or think about them?"

She laughed and responded, "No I did not know that, but now that you mention it, it certainly is the case and is most certainly true."

He then told her, "We've arrived."

They were now standing in front of a vast cave. Just inside, she could see several strange-looking twin beds without mattresses—shaped similarly to garden lounge chairs. Rather than cheap metal, these were made of sturdy wood, hand-carved at an angle so that the head of the bed was permanently raised higher than the foot of the bed. Worn cushions and quilts served as the mattresses.

"Take your pick," he offered, sensing her reluctance.

"I don't know," she admitted.

"Isn't this why you've come this far? To break through the not knowing of it all?"

"True," she said.

"Truth," he corrected her.

She thought his need to correct her had been unnecessary.

He then assured her, "My hope is to introduce you to Truth. She has shown me the way. Perhaps she will also show you the way."

"Truth is a woman?"

"Of course," he replied.

She was relieved that he'd mentioned another woman. Maybe she was as safe as she had been on the back of his motorcycle. Maybe she'd never been safer. *Haven't you always been exactly where you are?* her mind whispered.

The first step inside the cave was hers. And suddenly the moonlight was gone. He watched her choose which bed she would take. Not until then did he join her in the darkness. "May I dream next to you?" he asked.

"Yes, I hoped you would."

He chose the one next to hers and together they took positions on their separate upright beds. The cave was echoing their every movement. One-footstep, one-word, one-breath, seemed more profound inside the cave. There was a chill in the air and the coolness was welcoming.

"I hope she will help you," he told her.

"Truth?"

"Yes, Truth. We close our eyes now."

"Thank you," she quietly said to him before closing her eyes.

He, too, closed his eyes and then reminded her gently, "Remember, always lean into the curves. It will keep you safe."

She still had the blossomed twig—she held it close to her heart as she began to drift.

And then, they drifted together.

CHAPTER SIXTEEN

THE SENSATION BEFORE falling asleep is like no other. Floating as if resting above the Acheron River. The in-between phase of wakefulness and slumber, between knowing and not knowing exactly when sleep would occur. Or would it occur? Or would it be one of those eternal nights when she would be so tired that she couldn't possibly sleep? Her body was numbing but her mind was on fire. Ethereal fire. How could she sleep? Her body wanted it but her mind was too curious about what was ahead to fall asleep. She kept her eyes closed, attempting to respect her body's wishes to let all go and attempting to respect The Italian's wishes to dream together. She tried. She tried to rest. She tried to fall.

And then the sound of young women whispering distracted her even more. She opened her eyes and saw six women, younger than she and sensational looking. No blemishes, their skin the colors of ivory and chocolate. No woman was more beautiful than the other, but perhaps the most striking one of them had the darkest, richest skin she had ever seen. She looked like a perfectly-carved ebony figurine in motion. The queen of them all.

The Darkest Woman approached her, apologetic. "I'm sorry we didn't mean to wake you up."

"That's okay," she told her.

The other Five Beauties joined the Darkest Woman, surrounding her bed, playful and giggling. There was too much gaiety for her to be afraid.

The Darkest Woman asked, "Come with us?"

"Thank you for the offer, but I don't even know where you are going."

"To a palace," the Darkest Woman answered.

"I've never been to a palace before."

"Good, so you'll come. And he'll come too," the Darkest Woman said referring to the sleeping Italian.

Another one of the Five Beauties shook The Italian gently, awakening him.

It wasn't long thereafter that they all stepped outside of the cave together.

She couldn't understand why it was bright daylight outside the cave and that the break of dawn had already come and gone. She didn't think she had slept, but maybe she had, if just a little.

The Darkest Woman led the way to a group of white stallion racehorses. Two of the horses were strapped to a wheeled sulky. She and The Italian were placed in the sulky-for-two while the group of beauties got onto their horses. After which, the Darkest Woman continued to lead the way on horseback.

The white stallions galloped at racetrack speed and it was by far the fastest ride of her life. More exhilarating than all the roller-coasters and amusement park rides in America combined. She held onto The

Italian and he held her back. The racehorses were clearly in their element as they passed the few motor vehicles that were on the road. Curves were taken even faster than on the motorbike. She and The Italian naturally leaned into the curves together. The speed was so fast that the wheels of the sulky began to spark. And before they knew it, they had moved through an arched gate where an enormous palace could be seen. The Darkest Woman reined the horses back, forcing them to slow down to a trot against their will.

No one had spoken during the entire journey. She and The Italian were dropped off at the front door to the palace.

She went to thank the Darkest Woman first, but the woman told her, "You will do the same for me one day."

"I will?" she asked puzzled.

"If it is your will to help another, then you will." That was the last thing the Darkest Women said to her. She and her Five Beauties led the racehorses to a pool of water when the front door of the palace opened.

CHAPTER SEVENTEEN

IT SURPRISED HER that a Goddess would open the door herself, nonetheless, that's what she had done. The Goddess was the most radiant being she had ever laid her eyes on. Or, was she a being? Whatever she was, she was a life-size aura whose shape was that of an ordinary woman with ordinary features. Ordinary, if it weren't for the translucent glow the female shape emanated.

The Goddess welcomed them both so sweetly it sounded as if she were singing. And then somewhat abruptly The Goddess excused herself, pulling The Italian to a side palatial hallway. She could hear The Goddess whispering to him, "You usually come alone, why have you brought another person here? And a woman?"

The Italian answered, "She needs you. I feel her need, although I don't know precisely what her need is. If she chooses to tell me, I will listen. I believe it is you she needs, though, and not me. I am a mere intellectual who believes in greater things. You are the Greater Thing."

The Goddess was pleased with his answer and so when she returned, she entwined one Goddess arm with hers, which felt very much like an ordinary arm except for the warmth that was not derived from temperature. It was emotional warmth that began with her arm and led straight to the center of her heart. As this happened, her heart began to pulsate differently. A full peaceful and relaxed state was co-mingling with a fully vibrant and elated state.

The Goddess led her and The Italian through the palace of marble and stone adorned with heavenly paintings and sculptures of women from the beginning of time. She also noticed there were other live womanly shapes or female auras that appeared to be exact replicas of The Goddess. These Goddess Replicas with their translucent glows were talking with other guests in the palace who were relaying their innermost turmoil. Each Goddess Replica seemed to become the nationality and the precise race of the guests they were speaking with. There was one man from China speaking to a Goddess Replica through a hospital mask; he was frightened to take it off for fear he might catch someone else's disease. She heard The Chinese Goddess Replica respond to the man with tenderness, "You cannot catch someone else's disease, only your own."

She then saw a child from Africa in a wheelchair talking to an African Goddess Replica. And then she noticed so many others, young and old alike. There were those who possessed material wealth and those who possessed nothing at all. So many different nationalities and cultures—all in one palace. Many catastrophes were being spoken of, in many different languages. She began to count how many Goddess Replicas there were.

The Goddess interrupted her thinking. When she spoke, once again it sounded as if she were singing, "Don't bother counting, you can't count to infinity."

She then asked The Goddess, "Who are they all? Each and every one of them looks exactly like you."

"Accountants and dancers think too much about numbers and counting," The Goddess told her.

"How do you know I'm an accountant?"

The Goddess smiled, "Every Goddess who appears to be me, is me. Why be a Goddess if you don't have special powers to help every single being that asks for help? Or perhaps more to the point, why be a Goddess if you can't offer help to beings who need help but who don't even know how to ask?"

She looked around the palace again, and saw more Goddesses than she could count in all parts of the palace. There were hundreds of bright rooms and endless hallways. Each room was larger than the one that came before it. There were no crowds. There was enough room for everyone and there were enough Goddesses for everyone.

The Goddess sang, "Your mind must be still now, you must stop focusing on the unnecessary things. Only then will the unimportances fall away."

"I don't know how to do that."

"You know much more than your mind knows how to think. I suggest you try."

They continued walking together, The Goddess, The Italian and her. She tried to keep her mind still, but she kept seeing more Goddesses and more rooms and more people everywhere.

The Goddess interrupted her train of thought, "Why have you come here?"

She answered The Goddess with another question, "If you're a Goddess, shouldn't you already know?"

The Goddess looked directly into her, "I do know."

Once The Goddess looked into her eyes, her mind stopped wandering and all the other Goddesses and all the other people in the palace went away. All that remained in the palace was the three of them. It became so quiet that she began to feel and to hear her own heartbeat.

The Goddess commanded her, "Think your thoughts and I shall know them."

It wasn't hard for her to start thinking about him again. Real love. That was, he was, the only reason why she was there. Thoughts of him were always with her. She thought back to the moment they first met, at a business meeting, and how even though they didn't speak about it, there was immediate trust between them. They didn't know what kind of trust it was back then. It was real trust.

The Goddess spoke again, "You know you will see him again so why have you come this far?"

"I believe it, but I don't know it. I don't understand it. I don't have a clue as to how or when it will manifest, but I have a belief that I want certainty to. He was everything to me. And all the other things in this great life were better because of him. I was better because of him."

The Goddess spoke in song, "There is only one story, one road now. Now is left. There are signs in plenty that, being, is ingenerated and indestructible. That being is whole, unwavering and complete. Being is continuous."

The Italian interjected, "Change is illusion."

The Goddess affirmed his views, "Everything that is, always has been and always will be. You've been on this road many times."

She answered, "Yes, everything you say seems to be true and must be true, but how can I go on with my life when I do not understand?"

"Young woman, you do understand in a clearer way than clarity of the mind can ever bring you."

"You mean, clarity of the soul?" she asked.

"Repeat this back to me in song, and so when you return to the world you came from, you will remember me and your mind will not question what your soul tells you. Are you ready?"

She answered with hesitation but her answer was indeed, "Yes."

The Goddess sang, "Only one road, one story, now is left."

She repeated, "Only one road, one story, only now is left."

The Goddess sang again, "Only one road, one story, now is left."

She questioned The Goddess, "But that is the same thing you have already said and I have already repeated."

The Goddess insisted, "I want you to know these words as if they are a part of you. You will memorize them and take them back to the mundane world and you will teach it to others."

She questioned the word mundane, but all the

while she obediently repeated the words as spoken words first, and soon began to sing them as The Goddess had, "Only one road, one story, only now is left. Only one road, one story, only now is left."

The Goddess added, "Being is whole, unwavering and complete. Being is continuous."

She repeated each and every word back to The Goddess and in song. She repeated passages she didn't quite understand, "Hence all things are a name which mortals lay down and trust to be true—coming into being and perishing, being and not being, and changing place and altering bright color."

The Goddess sang more confusing verses aloud. All the while, she sang the verse back to The Goddess, "And since there is a last limit, it is completed on all sides, like the bulk of a well-rounded ball, equal in every way from the middle. For it must not be at all greater or smaller here or there."

Painstakingly she continued with each and every stanza The Goddess put forth while The Italian silently cheered her on. The last riddle she sang back was, "Look at things which, though absent, are yet present firmly to the mind; for you will not cut off for yourself what is, from holding to what is."

Once The Goddess was confident her memory was intact, she cautioned, "Now that you have learned, don't tell people to believe this because The Goddess says so. Tell them to work it out in their own minds and to see it for themselves. Do you understand?"

"Yes, I think so."

The Goddess then said, "Yet, you hesitate."

"I still don't know the answer to my own question. I need to know."

"You have all the knowledge you need. I cannot offer you more."

She stared at The Goddess, wanting, hoping for more, but she received nothing more.

The Goddess looked gently into her when she asked, "You'll remember the song when you return to the mundane world?"

"I hope so, but what if I can't remember every word? I certainly don't understand every word.

"You'll remember what you are meant to remember, you'll understand what you are..."

She completed The Goddess' last verse with her in harmony, "I'll understand what I am meant to understand."

She felt The Goddess' light shine through her.

Before she could thank The Goddess, the female figure had vanished. And the palace was empty; only she and The Italian remained.

The Italian told her, "We must leave now."

They walked together through the empty marble hallways, their echoes sounded much like their echoes inside the cave. The front door of the palace automatically opened for them.

Once they stepped outside, they continued well beyond the arched gates made of steel that automatically closed behind them.

Together they stood on the open terrain of Greece. This time, there was no river.

"What now?" she asked The Italian.

"You want to go back to Athens, don't you?"

"Of course," she told him.

He pointed south and said, "That is your road."

She looked ahead and all she could see was another empty road.

She thought to herself, only one road now, only one story, only now is left.

"And your road?" she asked.

"I will take another."

He turned to kiss her and she allowed it. She deepened it. Theirs was a sensual kiss that lingered. If this had occurred earlier, perhaps their story would be one story. But it was too late, she had gone too far and he knew too much about her. They both knew neither story, not his nor hers, would ever be complete as one.

They stood next to each other, two stories side by side. Stories that had briefly intersected. Neither wanted to say goodbye just yet.

The Italian initiated their separation first when he asked, "When you think of me, will you think of truth?"

She nodded her head.

And then he added, "And when I think of you, I will think of desire."

They each took their separate roads and neither of them chose to look back.

CHAPTER EIGHTEEN

SHE REALIZED SHE was still carrying the white-blossomed twig The Italian had given her and so she placed it inside the front pocket of her blouse. Only then did she dare to look at the open road to Athens. Another long arduous day was ahead of her. She wondered how long this one would last. Since she had arrived in Greece, each new day seemed to be longer than the day that had preceded it. And now, with every step she took, the road ahead just seemed to be getting longer.

This made her angry, which was not directed at anyone else other than herself. Why, when she had the opportunity, hadn't she asked The Italian or The Goddess for a pair of shoes so she could at least walk to Athens in less pain? Her feet had become calloused. There wasn't much blood, though there were traces of it.

Her anger began to heighten on remembering another question she should have posed to The Goddess. The question of Aristotle. She had gone straight to the point of Real Love, but it had completely slipped her mind to ask about The Thinker. Why, so far, had no one known about Aristotle when even people in America at least knew his name? If The Goddess was indeed all-knowing, then surely she would have known that she had come to Greece for concrete information about Aristotle. Therefore, why hadn't The Goddess told her anything about The Thinker, or at least guided her? It seemed unfair.

And was The Tourist in New York who told her about The Thinker crazy, or was she, The Tourist in Greece, the crazy one? It was all the more frustrating that every single person she had met in Greece had in one way or another been obsessed with dreaming rather than focusing on the here-and-now.

Her here-and-now was on a blistering road to Athens. Her skin was dry, as was her throat. She tried swallowing a few times when she became aware of a lingering taste of The Italian. She and The Italian had touched each other so briefly and yet his kiss and his smell were with her. She had no regrets about not going further, she certainly didn't want to turn around and go find him. The flavor in her mouth forced her think of him. And then she remembered what The Priestess told her and so she decided to give thanks to God or The Gods and now The Goddess for The Italian, and for the Six Beauties on horseback who had taken them to the palace. And whom would she thank for The Goddess? God, The Gods and The Goddess or The Goddesses? The uncertainty of how the higher sphere worked was daunting. She then also gave thanks to the Above Realm, wherever, whatever they were, for the weak fact that she forgot to ask about The Thinker, and then she also gave thanks for her sore feet.

Moving forward, she reminded herself what she had come for: *All women by nature desire to know.*

Not long thereafter, whether voluntarily or involuntarily, she sang these few notes as she went: *Only one road, one story, only now is left.*

She thought more and more about her experience with The Goddess and wondered why The Goddess had described the world as mundane. It seemed rather cruel in some ways. Was life mundane? Sometimes it seemed to be. Was having blisters on her feet mundane or was it simply a part of being alive. Blisters that would eventually heal was a sector of the ongoing world of beauty, not the opposite. Blisters separated her from Real Love. Real Love was now somewhere else without open wounds, a somewhere else she could not understand. She knew the sores on her feet would heal, but would her heart ever heal?

She swallowed again. At first it was the taste of The Italian but then it filtered into another dimension. That of Real Love. Suddenly she could taste Real Love's taste and she could smell his smell. It was far from mundane to be reminded of Real Love in all its configurations. Was he there with her on this empty road to Athens? She could sense him, or was it a chemical or mental reaction of being stuck on an endless road? She loved him, she thought. And then she rephrased the thought and then spoke her revision aloud.

To her one road she said, "I love him."

With this love, she was ready to go back to Athens, nothing would stop her and she would not take on one more distraction. She began to wonder how many days she had been gone. And would anyone have noticed how long she was gone? Would anyone have cared?

Had she alienated everyone she ever knew? She admitted the truth to herself finally. She was lost, in all its meanings. Simply and utterly lost. Strangely, she didn't mind being lost.

She breathed in the sweet scent of Real Love along with the majestic scent of the towering trees along the road. She was unable to identify them all but the tallest ones she recognized as cypresses and firs. She also saw there were trees bearing fruit. She saw pears, pomegranates and apples. She stopped at a fig tree and took just one piece of fruit that she immediately ate. The natural juice from the fig wet her dry throat. She kept walking, breathing everything in so deeply that before she knew it, her throat had become dry again. The rising heat and temperature were not helping. She tried to swallow more and more but this time, she began to cough. This did not stop her from moving forward. She coughed and kept walking ahead. And when she turned the very next corner, she was surprised to see she was stepping onto another Greek road. A motorway, infested with traffic and covered in a cloud of smog. It was a shock to her system to suddenly breathe in the polluted air, and more shocking that she was so close to Athens. The view and the road were clearly marked. Athens was straight ahead.

She figured if she kept walking at a steady pace, she could make it to the Greek City in an hour or so. Hard to know. The heat distorted her vision and her thinking. She could probably hitchhike. Back home hitchhiking alone was unthinkable, but here, all she had encountered thus far was genuine help. Nonetheless, she decided against it. Not that she was afraid of hitchhiking; she simply did not want another adventure. She was adventured-out. She was ready for a real city in a real bed. She preferred city life even though it went against the human instinct for nature. She tried swallowing again but the only result was more coughing. She was choking on the exhaust fumes of the city and yet she was eager to return to it.

It was then an old, pale blue car pulled up next her. The sputtering vehicle was a Plymouth Valiant. The Valiant was beat up and in desperate need of a mechanic; its engine screeched from under the hood. The Driver, a young guy maybe twenty years old, spoke to her in Greek. He was exceedingly polite, but she did not understand what he was saying. She simply responded with "No thank you," while she began to cough even more because of the Valiant's emissions. The Passenger tried handing her a bottle of Zagori. She could see it had already been opened and instinctively chose not to drink from it. The Passenger then took the cap off, drank directly from the bottle and then handed it to her. She took the bottle of Greek water and drank the whole thing in one go. It didn't take long. She then told him, "Thank you," and began to walk away. The Valiant drove along next to her as she walked.

The Driver spoke again, this time she understood what he said as he spoke in fluent English, "It's dangerous in our country for a woman to travel alone."

"It's dangerous in my country, too," she told him.

"May we at least escort you to safety? We will stop as you wish," The Driver insisted.

"I'll be okay."

"I am a born aristocrat. And although that does not deem me to be a good man, I was raised to be a gentle-man. It would not be just for me to leave you on the side of the road."

"You wouldn't be leaving me on the side of the road. I am already here, walking on it."

"Truth," The Driver said.

When she heard the word truth, it startled her. It made her think immediately of The Italian and The Goddess and how good they had been to her. The word truth, the plain and simple five letter word, brought up a grateful feeling inside her.

The Passenger then spoke for the first time, "Permit me to suggest—you need a ride."

The language and the rhythm in which The Passenger spoke was familiar to her. When she peered into the car to examine him, she saw a man who was probably close to her age. Not yet old, and no longer young.

"Thank you both," she said. And then she repeated, "I'll be okay." And yet she had stopped walking and the Valiant had also stopped moving.

The Passenger then offered, "Permit me to suggest—there is trust."

She leaned into the car, not afraid. She looked at The Passenger more closely and she could see he also wore no shoes. She asked, "How can there be trust when we don't know each other?"

"It is more important that we trust each other, rather than the importance of not trusting each other."

"We?" she asked.

The Passenger was deliberate in not answering her.

"Us?" she asked again.

"Society. If trust does not begin here, where can it begin?"

Her personal stance had remained—she still believed she had no fear and still believed she had no courage. She looked at the miles of motorway ahead and then decidedly reached her hand toward the back door handle, but The Passenger had already moved to the backseat. He left the front door wide open for her.

She rode next to The Driver on one long vinyl bench seat. It had been decades since she had been in such a sedan. It felt as large as her first New York apartment. The car must have been around since the nineteen-sixties. The old Valiant moved forward with three passengers and she was one of the three.

The Driver directed a question to both her and The Passenger in back, "Can either of you tell me the barometer for knowing or not knowing you are a just man?"

"Or a just woman?" she interjected.

The Driver continued, "Imagine yourself invisible."

"That's how it feels to be a woman sometimes."

"If invisible, would you still be a just man? Or a just woman? Would I have picked you up from the side of the road? I know my own personal answer, but do you know your own answers?"

She shrugged him off, and then told him, "I don't know. Maybe you're not meant to know the answer. Maybe you're thinking about it too much?"

The Driver answered, "Yes, it's something I've been known to do." And then he added, "Thinking is the talking of the soul with itself."

The Passenger leaned forward from the back, exclaiming, "To find yourself is to think for yourself!"

There was electricity between The Driver and The

Passenger. She couldn't quite put her finger on what their connection was. Were they relatives, father and son, or brothers? Lovers, perhaps. Whatever was between them, it was a real bond. Probably not dissimilar to Real Love, she imagined.

Not one of them said anything more on the subject of thinking. Thus she began to relax with the two strangers as the Valiant puttered forward. There was no air conditioning and the windows had been rolled down. The dashboard was lightening-hot just like the bottoms of her feet were only minutes ago. Her body was no longer over-heated, instead she felt simply hot. The breeze the old Valiant was generating as it moved forward was the answer to her prayer if she had said one.

The Driver asked, "Where have you traveled from?"

She didn't hesitate to tell them both about The Italian who had introduced her to The Goddess and how exciting it was to have met a Goddess. She also confided that her experience with The Goddess had been something of a letdown. She hadn't received the answer she had come for. Yes, she received personal attention from a heavenly figure, which exceeded her imagination, but she didn't know more than she knew before. She told them, everybody she'd met so far seemed preoccupied with dreams and not reality. And then she went backwards in telling them about her travels. She told them about The Old Man in the Park, her New Friend and The Priestess under the Oak Tree. She also told them about the fact that before she arrived, she never thought about music in the same way she did now. Now everything she did, everywhere she went, she heard music. For example, she began to explain, but she stopped herself from talking and instead began to sing to them.

Not necessarily in the order it was taught to her and modified as her memory dictated, she sang to them, "Change is illusion. Everything that is, always has been and always will be. You've, we've, been on this road many times. It is complete on all sides, a perfect sphere. Equal in every way from its center. It must not be at all larger or smaller in any direction. Being is whole, unwavering and complete, being is continuous. There is only one story, one road. Now is all that's left."

The Strangers both looked at each other, intrigued. The Driver shouted the name of "Parmenides" first, while The Passenger shouted just after, "Aletheia."

"I don't know them, I don't even know who they are," she said.

"But you do know them," The Passenger insisted.

"No, I know nothing about either of them."

The Passenger told her, enthusiastically, "Anytime, you hear the word truth or for that matter anytime you use the notion of truth in everyday conversation, it harks back to Parmenides because he invented it."

"Parmenides invented logic," The Driver added.

The Passenger went onto say, "And, Aletheia is none other than your Goddess."

The Driver was smiling when he added, "In our language, Aletheia means truth."

She hardly knew what to say. The two strangers had fire in their eyes whenever they spoke and for that matter they had fire in their eyes when they listened. Their fire was quickly becoming contagious. They spoke quickly and succinctly. What's more, everything they told her, they made sure it was highly accessible for her to comprehend. There was no pretension. It was plain and simple knowledge—an open range for the mind.

The Passenger said, "Permit me to ask, is your question of the scientific nature, or is your question of the personal nature?"

"Not scientific," she told him.

"You were courageous to come here," The Passenger commented.

"I'm not afraid, but I am certainly not courageous."

The Driver insisted, "Courage is knowing what not to fear."

It was then she decided it was safe to ask, "Do either of you know anything about Aristotle?"

Both Strangers stared straight ahead at the open road. Neither of them answered or acknowledged her question.

She was astounded nobody in Greece had yet to engage with her in a conversation about Aristotle, or seemed to have any interest at all. Why, she wondered?

The Passenger disrupted her train of thought when he asked, "What will you do next to attain your answer?"

"I don't know, but I'll stop at nothing."

"Bold and courageous," The Driver reiterated.

She thought back to The Old Man in the Park, at Plato's Academe, and she remembered what he had told her. She decided to repeat The Old Man's words, "I'll do anything, everything to know, knowing I may never know."

The Passenger leaned forward again, this time

more tender than fiery when he asked, "Have you tried Kledones?"

With a wryness she responded, "I don't have to take a magic carpet to get there do I?"

The Passenger laughed, "No, but I would think it to be enjoyable to take a magic carpet." And then he became more serious. "Kledones is another form of divination that will not take you off your grid."

CHAPTER NINETEEN

THERE WERE NO stops or turns and the closer The Valiant Men and she got to Athens, the slower the traffic became. The Passenger had assured her that The Agora would be the best place for Kledones and that it was only a stone's throw from her hotel. "Anywhere there is a fairly large gathering of people, where crowds of people roam, there is potential to receive a profound answer from the divine. All anyone need do is listen."

The Driver told them, "I intend to wait in the car."

"You will join us," was The Passenger's only response.

The Driver insisted, "There are too many varieties of germs and viruses in public spaces, I prefer not to expose myself to any contagious strain. Unless, of course, it is deemed imperative."

"Nonsense. Paranoia and hypochondria are self-imposed. This woman's needs are our needs. She is our deemed imperative."

The Driver shook his head, and then looked at the overcast sky above, "If nothing else, the Nefos will kill us."

"Nefos?" she asked.

"Smog can irritate your condition, but it cannot kill you. Be patient and let the Meltemi carry it away," The Passenger assured him.

"There is no Meltemi," The Driver said with uncertainty.

"There will be," The Passenger said with certainty and then added, "The Meltemi always comes. The dry northern winds always carry the smog away."

The Valiant drove deep into the rush hour of Athens. The old sedan never stopped moving until they reached The Agora, which turned out to be nothing more than a crowded outdoor market. Every legal and illegal parking space, including in front of all the fire hydrants and on top of every sidewalk, was already taken. The Valiant circled The Agora a few times and then The Driver decidedly headed straight for a brick staircase, driving up a portion of the stairs and parking the old car.

As they got out of the sedan, The Passenger whispered one word to her, "Aristocrats."

A Woman With A Camera watched them as they left the vehicle on the staircase. The Woman swiftly followed, asking The Passenger specifically, "Are you who I think you are?"

The Passenger was polite when he answered, "Best to concentrate on who you are and not who I am."

The Woman asked if she could take a photograph of him, and when he politely declined, she took a series of pictures of The Three of them anyway as they headed towards The Agora.

None of The Three discussed the Woman With A Camera; instead, The Passenger excitedly placed his hands over his ears, instructing them both, "Now. We cover our ears until we are well into the crowd. Once we uncover our ears, the first random utterance we hear should be God's answer to our question."

The Driver added one word, "Theoretically."

The Passenger kept his focus. "We must now ask our own question silently and privately. We must now concentrate."

She placed her hands over her ears and then The Driver reluctantly followed suit.

The Three of them together, side by side by side, walked into the dense crowd of The Agora filled with buyers and sellers. With their hands over their ears, every substantial sound was muted. She had never been to a market without sound; it was a quiet symphony of hustle without the bustle. They walked among stands of every Mediterranean product conceivable: Fruits and vegetables, flowers and plants and herbs, fish and meat and spices, soaps and sea sponges, honey and olives and olive oil, linens, clothing, ivory, handbags, belts and shoes. And there were people, crowds and crowds of people—more exotic than her imaginings.

The Three continued together, still covering their ears while weaving through the labyrinth. They passed by musicians, but she couldn't hear what they were singing. They passed by more than one beckoning gypsy with decks of cards and crystal balls. There were old women and children with over-sunned, over-wrinkled hands stretched out, begging for money with their eyes. Every nationality seemed to be present. A United Nations gathering without a committee.

The Passenger continued to lead them, until they arrived at what seemed to be the most crowded part of The Agora and what seemed to be the center. She thought to herself in no particular order, "A perfect sphere, I've, we've been on this road many times. It is complete on all sides, equal in every way from its center. It must not be at all larger or smaller in any direction."

She spun herself around looking in all directions of The Agora. The Three of them were indeed in its center.

She hadn't forgotten The Passenger's instructions, and so she contemplated her burning question once again. It was a pleasure. *Real Love.* Love was the only thing that ever gave her any strength. It seemed any other emotion was depleting. Love was everything and so she thought about her question one more time. As deeply as ever she sang these words to herself: *Will I ever see him again? I believe I will, but I don't know. I want to know. I need to know. Please let me know.*

The Passenger pulled them into a circle of Three so that they faced each other, saw each other, acknowledged each other, trusted each other before claiming their answers. Once he was satisfied that they were in unity, he released his hands from his ears, and then she and The Driver did the same.

A cacophony of sound set in. Not one single sound, but the sounds of voice and movement and machinery colliding. They broke from their huddle, heading together in the opposite direction from where they had come, ready for their Divine Answers. The first distinct sound she heard was a tapping. Tap, tap, tap. She searched for the sound with her eyes until she could see a Young Blind Man with a white cane. She watched The Young Blind Man tap his way through the crowd until he and the sound were gone. Then came a churning sound; her eyes found the sound, which was solid ice being crushed into particles. She then heard a woman's voice and turned around to see and hear—a Woman in Bright Colors of silk was speaking in an unknown language, perhaps she was Syrian. None of The Three knew this language. They kept moving forward, and then they heard a Man's Voice. Another unknown language, an Egyptian man, perhaps. If The Egyptian carried the Divine Answer, they would never know what it was. An African dialect was heard, but again, none of The Three understood this message.

It was then they heard an overpowering voice, talking above all the other voices. The Three turned to this voice, a Young Greek Man talked abrasively on his cell phone. He spoke with vigor when he said, "S'agapo" but then he repeated it, louder, "S'agapo" and then he moved past them continuing on his cell phone, the balance of his words inaudible.

The Valiant Men turned to her and asked if she knew what "S'agapo" meant?

"What does S'agapo mean?" she asked with hope and without fear.

The Passenger was pleased to translate for her, "I love you."

The Driver added, "S'agapo has many meanings, it could be love for anybody. A lover, a brother, a childhood friend, anybody."

"Is that all?" she asked.

The Passenger was excited. "One word frees us of all the weight and pain in life. That word is Love."

"That is not what I came for, I know about Love."

The Passenger said to her, "Then you have everything you'll ever need."

"I don't have it anymore."

The Passenger then understood. "So you have come to find Love again?"

The Driver told him, "Of course that's why she has traveled so far. Is there any other reason?"

The Driver looked at The Passenger and then repeated the words to him, "S'agapo."

Her eyes began to well up, as she could see there was love between the two of them. Whatever it was, she knew it was not her business to pry, but she could feel it between them. She was not filled with envy, it was more of a yearning. An eternal seeking that began the moment of Real Love's departure. She began to feel faint. The Driver picked her up and carried her to the shade where The Three of them sat together on a park bench. The trees rustled above and as The Passenger had predicted, the dry winds started to pick up.

She looked up at the sky and although she could not see the wind, she could feel it. And so she asked with one word, "Meltemi?"

And the Driver answered with another word, "Truth."

And so The Three of them sat on the bench, she between The Valiant Men, experiencing the wind they could not see. The Three observed The Agora, the buyers and sellers and wanderers, but none of The Three wanted to be inside The Agora. They watched and listened and were content in their own private silences. Not one of them asked the other what their personal question was for the Divine, although somehow without asking, they sensed they knew each other's questions. It was an unexpected unity she felt with The Valiant Men who didn't seem to be interested in her body as much as her soul. She liked this feeling, for it made her feel safe.

CHAPTER TWENTY

THE NEFOS ABOVE the city of Athens was lifting, just as The Passenger said it would. The skies were clearing, which helped her lungs and her mind. The market was also beginning to clear, winding down for the night. The dismantling of booths and tables and stands and chairs began while boxes of produce were being sold-off for a fraction of what the price had been only moments before. She could see a handful of locals, buyers, who had been waiting for the bargains of the closing ceremonies. Trucks and other vehicles arrived in order to cart-away unsold merchandise, while a group of old women used donkeys to take away their unsold goods. Dusk was on its way.

She had the feeling she never wanted the day to end, while conversely feeling that she wanted the day to end immediately. For if the day went on forever, she would be forever surrounded by two men who believed in what she believed in—the unabashed pursuit of knowledge. The desire for real knowledge, where Real Love is the only thing that matters. And yet if the day were to come to its immediate end, it could put a halt to her endless desire. If it turned out there was no end in sight, she imagined she could stay hopeful for the rest of her entire life. That, she didn't want. She didn't want to be fixated on empty hope. She only wanted a real result. And there was only one result she wanted in the end. After all, *all women by nature desire to know*, and when she looked at The Valiant Men, she thought to herself as Aristotle had once thought, *all men by nature desire to know*.

Before she could say anything on the subject, it was The Passenger who decided to speak his mind first. "Permit me to assume—you did not get the answer you came for."

"Truth," she said.

The Passenger sighed, and then told her the following: "My Guardian Angel never gives me the guidance I want. She never tells me what to do. All she does is tell me what not to do. If I am turning right, I will hear her say, 'No!' If I am about to drink from the well, I will hear her say, 'No!' If I have chosen to go home early instead of working late, she will command, 'No!' I yearn for the day that once, if only once, she tells me an action to take rather than an action not to take."

"You know your Guardian Angel?"

"She's never presented herself to me, except for her clear voice above all other voices negating whatever I try to do. Indeed, she does protect me and she's always been right. Many have said it's merely a condition of the mind, mental, or a strand of schizophrenia. Yet I know she speaks only what is true."

"And you have no proof other than what you believe?"

"None."

"That's how I feel about my question," she confessed. "I feel I know what the answer is, or at least I know what I want the answer to be. Either way, there is no concrete proof."

"Proof about love?" asked The Passenger.

"Proof relating to the eternity of love," she admitted.

And then it was The Driver who spoke. "Every heart sings a song, incomplete, until another heart whispers back. Those who wish to sing always find a song. At the touch of a lover, everyone becomes a poet."

She breathed in his each and every word, deeply.

The Driver was not delicate when he told her, "You may very well spend the rest of your life without obtaining proof."

"I can't live with that," she told them.

The Driver added, "People live with all sorts of restrictions: physical, mental, financial. Some choose their personal restrictions while other restrictions are inflicted. You can continue on forever with your quest if you so desire."

"I only desire one thing. To know."

Her relentlessness intrigued them both. The Driver said, "Human behavior flows from three main sources: desire, emotion, and knowledge."

"So you see, I am right to stop at nothing."

The Driver then pointed to The Passenger. "He believes that wisdom consists in knowing that you do not know. I too believe that and I will spend my life trying to perpetuate it. I believe in this wisdom and yet I also equally believe in questions."

The Passenger interjected, "Questions can be as

powerful as the answers we are looking for."

The Driver continued on, "Questions have the ability to induce a mental state of aporia, which encourages people to find out what they want to know for themselves. Aporia turns us all into desirous beings, willing to investigate the truth."

She quoted Aristotle's words to them, "All women by nature desire to know."

The Passenger smiled at that and added to it by saying, "Woman once made equal to man becomes his superior."

This made her laugh. She had not remembered having laughed for quite some time in her measurement of time.

The Passenger spoke again, "For wisdom is a most beautiful thing, and Love is of the beautiful; and therefore Love is also a philosopher or lover of wisdom, and being a lover of wisdom is in a mean between the wise and the ignorant."

The Driver added, "Philosophers are the troublemakers of our time."

The Three laughed together.

"Oh!" she said, "I heard this from an Old Man in a Park not far from here. Tell me what you think. He told me, 'There is only one good: knowledge and...'"

The Passenger completed her sentence for her, "And one evil: ignorance."

"And then The Old Man in the Park told me to lie down on the rocks to sleep. He said, 'Permit me to suggest—you need to sleep.'"

The Passenger asked, "And did you? Lie down on the stones?"

"Yes." Then she observed The Passenger more

closely. She saw he resembled The Old Man in the Park, but at an earlier age. Or perhaps The Old Man in the Park was his relative. Was it too coincidental or non-coincidental that there might be a connection, she wondered. They looked into one another's eyes. Did he feel the same way? Did he feel he might know her from before, or did he think he somehow recognized her? Why and how did they have such a bond, when she was nothing more than a tourist, or moreover, a reluctant hitchhiker? The intonation in his voice also held familiarity.

The Passenger told her, "For God mingles not with man, but through Love. All the intercourse, and converse of God with man, whether awake or asleep, is carried on. The wisdom which understands this is spiritual."

She thought it was one of the most beautiful things she had ever heard. But then almost everything the two of them had to say was the most beautiful thing she had ever heard. And then she asked The Passenger, "Have I met you before? Or maybe I met your father, you remind me of someone who helped me once."

He smiled into her while he answered with another question, "Have you mistaken me for someone else?"

"No, I don't believe I have."

"Maybe I came to you in a dream?"

She laughed again, "Or maybe I came to you in my dream."

He did not laugh, but he enjoyed listening to her speak her thoughts with abandon.

She turned to The Driver, "So, it was his idea to bring me here to The Agora for the Kledones. Do you have a suggestion as to where I should go next?"

The Driver was not as encouraging when he said, "Objects of knowledge are not in this world." As he constructed his thoughts internally, he reached his hand skyward, "Knowledge is sometimes up above in the realm of forms and patterns we cannot see. They are not of this world, they are only in our mind."

"I don't understand."

"We all know what a circle is, correct?"

"Yes, of course."

"But have we seen one?"

"Everyone has."

"Incorrect." The Driver extracted a gold coin from his pocket and handed it to her. It looked to be an ancient coin, one she had never laid her eyes on before. She held onto it while he asked, "Now, is that a circle?"

"Yes," she answered.

He corrected her, "No, it is not. The edges are imperfect. It is not an equal distance from the center out to all points of the edge. But we all perceive it to be a circle. This is no true circle as you can confirm, if you so happen to feel its imperfect shape."

She ran her fingers along the imperfect edges of the ancient coin while staring at the face of it—an image of a woman who appeared to be a Goddess. "Who is she?"

"Athena—Goddess of our city." He flipped the coin so that she could to view its opposite side that depicted an owl. "Athena with the owl's open wings and with the olive leaves tells the world our city is powerful, victorious and peace-loving."

"And that circles don't exist."

"Not down here on earth they don't, but up

somewhere in a realm we don't understand, perfect circles most certainly exist."

"Are you saying that I will never find the true answer to my question?"

"Not at all. I only mean to say that the knowledge you are looking for may have no rationality to it, and yet it could still hold truth."

"I'm not sure this is helping me. In fact, I'm finding it more confusing than helpful."

The Driver explained, "Reason can only take you so far, sometimes truth has to come down and set you aflame."

"I think I'd like that."

The Passenger interjected, "Sometimes, that's what we live for."

"So then, is there no place I can go for my answer?" she asked.

The Valiant Men considered this while looking at the other, taking in her question. The two of them then talked over each other. The Passenger answered, "It is quite probable that you have already obtained your answer."

While at the same time The Driver answered, "There are hundreds of places you can go to ask your question. Now whether the truth can be found in any of those places, or not, is another matter."

The Valiant Men both ended the discussion by saying, "Neither of us can say that we know."

The temperature in her body began to rise, while her state of euphoria by meeting the two of them began to wane. Listlessness set in. They had stimulated her and had given her hope while at the same time, they absolutely could not fortify her. It worried her to think her journey was near its end. Its empty end. Sadness washed over her. If not emptiness.

The Agora had emptied as well. The only people left were The Unwanteds: street cleaners and beggars and scrappers and alley cats were taking care of any debris left. As nighttime emerged, the street lamps came on and young people with cigarettes and bottles of alcohol came onto the scene in small clusters. Night musicians in search of donations also appeared. And even though this was not the elite of Athens, an elite quality arrived with the nightfall. All the people milling through the empty marketplace were focused and seemed to be hard-working, whether what they were doing could be considered work or not. It was unity amongst strangers. Everybody there had shown up with some kind of hope for their evening ahead. She hoped for all the people there, that their hope was not as empty as hers.

Not a fraction of daylight was left when a Round Man approached their bench. He seemed to be neither a happy man nor a sad one. Perhaps the Round Man was earnest. He stepped in front of The Passenger and asked, "Sir, will you be speaking tonight by any chance?"

The Passenger told him, "No, not tonight."

The Round Man asked, "Is there anything you can at least say that will lift my spirits? I don't want to be a nuisance, but if there was anything on your mind, it would be a great honor to hear it."

The Passenger asked, "Do you know of my eighteen-ities?"

"I wish I could say I knew of them, but I do not," the Round Man admitted.

The Passenger then stood up. He spoke in a raised voice as if a world-class actor as he addressed the man, "Serenity, regularity, absence of vanity. Sincerity, simplicity, veracity, equanimity. Fixity, non-irritability, adaptability. Humility, tenacity, integrity, nobility, magnanimity, charity, generosity, purity. Practice daily these eighteen-'ities.' You will soon attain immortal-ity."

The Round Man soaked it in, and then laughed, a gigantic belly laugh that seemed to echo throughout The Agora and back. Onlookers she hadn't noticed before began to applaud while the Round Man told him, "Thank you, thank you very much indeed. You have lifted my spirits in a way I truly hadn't expected." The Round Man went on his way while The Passenger remained standing. Some of the Onlookers lingered in the shadows, hoping to hear more from The Passenger.

Her heart sank when she saw this because she knew her time with him and them was about to come to an end. The Driver stood up as well, confessing, "I would love to attain a fraction of his wisdom one day."

The Passenger responded with, "Wisdom begins in wonder."

It was full-on nighttime and Athens was electrified. She could see the outline of the city and when she looked across The Agora, she thought she could see her hotel. She also thought she could see a Starbucks alight in the near distance.

She figured she could go with the two of them, but there would be others now. Could she share them? Yes. Did she want to? No.

The Driver asked, "Would you like to come with us?"

"You are welcome to continue with us," The Passenger said.

"In many ways I want to go with you both, but I have to be strict with myself—I don't want to live in empty hope. I want the answer I came for. I want to complete my journey. I need to."

She handed the gold coin back to The Driver, but he stopped her, "Keep it, you might need it."

"But this coin must be extremely valuable," she told him.

"It only has value if it is used. Please, keep it."

She accepted and then asked, "So you are not going to give me any hint of where I should go next?"

The Passenger advised her, "Go anywhere you desire. Although permit me to suggest—do not stay stationary. It is dangerous for a woman to be alone in The Agora after nightfall."

The Driver then advised, "Let your questions be your guide and follow your boldness anywhere it should lead you. That said, let your boldness lead you anywhere but to Trophonius."

"What's Trophonius?"

"The Oracle of Trophonius is where only people at the end of their ropes go when they cannot find their answer any other way. It is dangerous, for women and men alike."

"What kind of danger?"

"Danger of the mind. Severe depression. It can leave anyone who dares go with long periods of delirium and babbling."

"Why would anyone go there?"

"Because they can't obtain what they want any other way. Because they are desperate. You seem to be eager but not desperate, so I trust your boldness will not take you there."

"And do these people who go to Trophonius ever recover?"

The Driver hesitated. "Eventually."

They were interrupted when an Onlooker, a woman, stepped between them to get closer to The Passenger and then another woman did the same. Several men appeared as well. More and more people began to gather around them. To her, the pushing and shoving felt overwhelming. To them, it seemed to be natural. The growing crowd began to separate her from them. It made her nervous, and then again, she was not afraid.

The Driver could see this when he said, "Courage is a kind of salvation."

The Passenger then spoke one last word to her. That word was "Love."

Because of the ever-growing crowd, she had become completely separated from them. She could see The Passenger and The Driver walking ahead, being followed by more and more people who wanted to be close to them. She could hear The Passenger speaking to the moving crowd, though his precise words were inaudible. She watched them continue to walk forward with abundantly more people joining their every step. She watched The Passenger and The Driver until they turned a street corner, where they disappeared into the night with a following.

CHAPTER TWENTY-ONE

SHE STOOD THERE in the silence of the park where The Three had just been together. Now, whatever The Three had between them was gone. Over. There were no wise words being spoken anymore. The only sounds she could hear were coming from The Agora and from the center of her heart. She could feel her heart pounding or beating—was there a difference? Courage, she thought. Love, she felt. *Dangerous for a woman to be alone in The Agora after nightfall*, The Passenger had said. But then her hotel was on the other side of The Agora. She could walk through The Agora, or around it. Either way, she was not afraid. Whatever she did, The Passenger advised her not to stay stationary and that seemed to be excellent advice and more than likely what she would have done anyway. Keep moving ahead, she thought. And so she took one step toward her hotel.

She walked along the outer rim of The Agora that had ample streetlight where she could appreciate the night creatures—and at a distance from any danger. She didn't think about getting back to her hotel as much as she thought about the fact that she missed them. Both of them: The Driver and The Passenger. She hadn't missed any living soul in her measurement of time except for Real Love, who she didn't need to remind herself was no longer living. It was a relief to her that she had succeeded in having a here-and-now emotion rather than a long-gone emotion. Except that The Driver and The Passenger were now gone, too. Not in a tragic way, but in a way that had left an imprint on her whole being. It was a different kind of missing than missing Real Love and it was a different kind of love. It was a different kind of fulfillment and melancholy that enveloped her. She hadn't expected this and as she walked she conjured up their images in her mind: The Driver, the young one, was the tallest and muscular and well-dressed, while The Passenger, who was less dramatic to the eye, wore a brown suit and was barefoot just as she was. She wondered why she hadn't asked The Passenger about his bare feet and why he hadn't asked her about hers either. Then she stopped to peer down at her own feet. There was no pain whatsoever, but they needed a good soaking. A hot bath in her hotel room was the most appealing thought she had entertained since her arrival in Greece.

She picked up her pace, imagining a luxurious bath, when she felt a presence behind her. Someone, whoever it was, was walking too closely behind. She crossed to the other side of the road to lose this presence, but whomever it was stayed with her and the footsteps that were following were coming much too close. This did not frighten her, rather, she turned around to confront the presence, which turned out to be a young Greek kid who towered over her and then pushed her.

While regaining her balance, she asked, "What do you want?"

"The gold coin," he answered with a rough voice.

"It was a gift, and even if it weren't a gift, you can't have it," she replied.

He pushed her again, and then, she pushed him back. She had never pushed anyone in her entire life. The moment she pushed him, he pushed her back, harder. He grabbed one of her arms and held it too tightly.

"How dare you!" she said. "A woman on her own without anything but one gold coin, and you want to have it and you'll hurt me in order to get it?"

"I want it and I will stop at nothing." The Kid pushed her again while twisting her arm behind her body.

She told him, "Over my dead body."

He answered, "As you wish." And he pulled out a knife.

She stared at the blade and then told him, "Nothing frightens me more than not seeing Real Love again. Do you understand that? Nothing."

He was confused, but didn't budge. Only his grip tightened.

Even with The Kid wielding a knife straight at her, she grabbed his wrist without one ounce of fear. She then twisted his arm the exact same way he was twisting hers. Her grip was also strong, to the point where he surrendered his knife instantaneously. It was not her strength that made The Kid give up his blade; it was sheer astonishment.

She held the knife toward him, copying his moves. "Now apologize."

"You're kidding."

"Nope, say you're sorry."

The Kid hesitated and then said it. "I'm sorry."

"Like you mean it."

"Okay, I'm sorry." And he ran off.

She kept the knife and decided to take the fast route to her hotel, that being straight through The Agora. And she never looked back.

The nightlife inside the market was not as fiercely interesting as it was from the outside. Nobody was interested in her and she was interested in nobody. She headed for the closest trashcan and immediately began extracting soiled newspapers and cartons from it. Her hands reached past the day's rotted fruits and vegetables to get exactly what she wanted. To any Onlooker, she would have appeared to have the quality of a night creature herself. She wrapped the knife many times over in the filthy materials she collected, and then buried the knife at the bottom of the debris. Her hands and arms were covered in a moist concoction of smelly rubbish, reeking of the sourest of odors.

She walked over to a water fountain, where she rinsed her hands and arms and then splashed water along her face and neck. Once she looked up, she could see her hotel more vividly. She walked toward it thinking again of a hot bath.

On leaving The Agora on the other side, she noticed a Tour Bus under a broken streetlamp. Long lines of people were waiting to board. She didn't give it much attention until she crossed the street and caught a glimpse of the front of the Tour Bus. Large letters marked the destination at the top of the windshield: Temple of Fortune, Oracle of Trophonius.

Unlike every other group or individuals she had encountered thus far in Greece, these people were not harmonious; there was no unity. These were somber individuals who happened to be boarding a bus together. There was no talk amongst one another, no exchanges. These were hard faces, engulfed in sadness. Not with the twinge of the romantic sadness that consumed her having to do with Real Love. Their sadness was another kind, one she did not know. Hopelessness was in the air. But then there must have been some kind of hope because all these forlorn people were going somewhere for help.

She found herself in front of a makeshift booth where a nondescript man sold tickets under the shadows. She asked when the next bus to Trophonius was scheduled to leave. He indicated there would not be another bus for quite some time. She inquired as to whether quite-some-time was measured in days or in weeks, but all he did was extend the palm of his hand out for her fare. She could see The Plaka right in front of her and could also see her hotel with the hot bath now closer to realization than before. And then she saw that all the people who had been waiting in line were now seated passengers on the bus. The Tour Bus Driver had started his engine. She looked at her gold coin, and then placed it in the palm of the ticket-seller's hand. The coin quickly disappeared inside the clutch of his hand.

She rushed to present her ticket to the Tour Bus Driver, and the doors closed right behind her. The Tour Bus began to move before she could find a seat. She searched until she found the last empty seat, next to a window. She climbed over the long legs of an unmoving man and then sank into the one last seat, which was broken. As they drove past her hotel and her hot bath, she took a deep breath and thought of The Valiant Men—The Driver and The Passenger—and she wondered what they would think. She imagined answering to them, "I must do everything to know." And she knew their response would be, "Knowing you may never know." But The Three of them were in sync and so she took another deep breath and looked at the road ahead. *There is only one story, one road now. Only now is left.*

If she were to guess, they were heading northeast. She started to ask the Long-Legged Man next to her, but decided against it. He seemed lost like everyone else on the bus. And she was lost with them. There was no spoken unity, no laughter, no communication. She then thought of her New Friend and what he had told her, "Music is the key to everything." And so the silence of everyone's thoughts and the churning of the buses' wheels became the music. And then she thought of her New Friend's Mother's utterances, *'All is One'* which seemed to play along with the music as the wheels took them down another road.

The music helped her to relax and she thought back to the last time she had been on a long bus ride. It was with him. Real Love. It was on New York's Chinatown bus to Boston, The Lucky Star, that had transported them for fifteen dollars apiece. It was pouring rain on that trip; the ride was long, well over four hours. It hadn't seemed long and it was on that rainy bus ride where he was the one stuck in a broken seat. And he never complained. The thought of that made her vow not to complain either, not even to herself. She imagined him. She imagined them. She imagined his hand taking hers and tucking it between his two hands, holding it on his lap for almost the entire journey. Sometimes they spoke incessantly, sometimes words were not necessary. Riding the bus together was as close to making love as anything. Everything they did together was a form of lovemaking. Standing in grocery store lines, folding laundry, washing dishes, borrowing each other's money, or rather giving each other money. Whoever had the most each month would instinctually give the other whatever sum they had. They kept nothing for themselves. But, they weren't always in harmony: there were headaches, heartaches, and the daily pain of being alive. And that's what making love remedied. Making love in any form whether sexual, spiritual, mental, metaphysical, tangible, imaginable was the plane where imbalances became balanced. That's what love was. Real Love existed no matter what the daily or nightly storyline was. Whether it was a day of success, a night of despair, or the variations in-between, love trumped every lack and disappointment.

She could feel him now, in her broken seat, alone. Real Love. Was she simply imagining him, remembering him, or was he there? She could feel his breath on her neck and his scent evoked chills all along her body. She breathed him in as long as it lasted, while the sound of the wheels of the bus and other people's silent yearnings lulled her into believing it real.

CHAPTER TWENTY-TWO

MAGNIFICENT SUNLIGHT was streaming atop the quaint town of Livadeia when the Tour Bus arrived. The ancient river Herkyna ran straight through its only restaurant—although the establishment was closed. Waterfalls and waterwheels graced the premises while animals roamed freely along the mountainous slopes. Wild herds of cows, sheep and mountain goats grazed contentedly. As there were no fences in sight, neither animal life nor plant life was segregated, therefore all the wildlife thrived together.

At the top of an isolated hill she could see a small chapel reflecting light, and that was where The Temple of Fortune and The Oracle of Trophonius were supposed to be. There was nothing ominous about the atmosphere, contrary to the never-go-there legend. She supposed that rumors were generated the same way in Greece as they were in the United States. The gossip equivalent to truth: If you hear a rumor twice, it must be true.

She and her Fellow Bus Companions were handed sack lunches, each filled with a Greek sandwich, a souvlaki, along with a pear, a bottle of Zagori and one honey-cake. She and her Fellow Bus Companions sat on a grassy incline overlooking the Herkyna's river-bank where they ate their meals in silence. She noticed that no one, not one person, had tasted their honey-cake. Every single person, including the Tour Bus Driver, had set his or her honey-cake aside. And so, even though she was yet to taste her very first honey-cake, she kept hers aside as her Fellow Companions had done.

The setting was idyllic and the food was fresh and the country air equilibrated her lungs and her senses. Sadly to her, none of this natural beauty seemed to raise the general mood a fraction above morose.

Just along the riverbank, she saw that a group of young boys were chasing a lone sheep. It was playful for the animal and the boys. Seemingly harmless until one of the boys finally caught up with the sheep and then took hold of it. Another boy handed a butcher knife to the boy who caught the sheep while the rest of boys quickly formed a circle around them. One boy held the sheep down while The Boy with the butcher knife quickly slit the sheep's neck wide open. A wailing sound from the dying sheep was momentary because the sound of the boys cheering overrode the sheep's cries. She had tried turning her head, but she had not been quick enough. She had seen it all, and a pool of blood lay on the earth. The Boy lifted his knife and then stabbed it again into the sheep's midsection where he began carving the stomach area until he came across a small organ, which he extracted. She wasn't sure what it was, but she was pretty sure it was not the sheep's heart because she imagined what the heart of a sheep would look like. Perhaps it was the sheep's liver. The Boy raised what she guessed was the sheep's liver, high and then ran with it across the river and disappeared.

She felt nauseous and, against her better judgment, she decided to look inside the bread of her sandwich. Unrecognizable meat, whether sheep or another kind of animal, she could not take another bite. Most of her Fellow Bus Companions had finished their meals and had bowed their heads down, whether praying or meditating or simply yearning she could not be sure.

No more than ten minutes later, The Boy who had killed the sheep reemerged, now without the sheep's liver. He continued to run as urgently as before, as he crossed back over the river and towards the Group of Bus Companions. The Boy spoke first to the Tour Bus Driver and then headed for the Long-Legged Man who she sat next to on the bus. She didn't understand much except that, based on the liver of the sheep, The Priests of Trophonius had determined it was his time. The Boy escorted the Long-Legged Man down to the river. The only thing the Long-Legged Man took with him was his honey-cake. Now that he was gone, her Fellow Bus Companions ate their honey-cakes. She watched the Long-Legged Man as he was greeted by another young boy. The Two Boys took off his clothing and took him into the deepest part of river to wash his body. She assumed it was a type of baptism—although she didn't believe in such things.

The Long-Legged Man was then led out of the river, and then The Two Boys wrapped him in white linen, winding the material tightly around his body. Once the preparation of the shroud was complete, The

Two Boys sent the man up the hill alone. The only thing he took with him was his honey-cake. He walked up the hill into the dark chapel. And then, the Long-Legged Man vanished inside The Temple of Fortune.

Where she and her Fellow Bus Companions remained was similar to summer camp, and it was all very organized: they slept in sleeping bags at the bottom of the hill, they were given meals, they were allowed short walks but were not allowed to stray too far. The attendants of Trophonius instructed each of them that whatever techniques they learned there could not be taken back to society. Whether written or oral, there would be no revealing of any sacred practices. They were encouraged of course to hold onto the wisdom they would learn, but they were required to take a vow not to give away any trade secrets of Trophonius. Not dissimilar to back home in Corporate America where nondisclosure agreements had become a standard requirement. As an accountant, she'd had to sign confidentiality contracts so many times. She took the Trophonius private practices vow along with everyone else.

Most days another lone sheep was sacrificed. It was a maximum of one killing per day, when the liver was extracted and presented to The Priests of Trophonius who, as she found out, would read the sheep's liver. They believed the sheep's liver was the shiniest organ of all mammals. Moments after a fresh slaughter, the sheep's liver was as glossy as a mirror where The Priests could peer into its reflective surface and receive divine guidance as to who would be next to consult with The Oracle of Trophonius.

She wanted to leave, go back to Athens and then

take the first flight back home. She'd had enough. She was not afraid of The Oracle of Trophonius, but the sheep's killings, the blood and the sounds frightened her. Her eyes never wandered towards the slaughtering again, but the first image had already been burned into her memory and replayed itself over and over again. The gore and the morbidness of it all had begun to live inside her. She didn't want to take one sheep's life to benefit her own.

After dark, under the moonless sky when the only light above came from the stars, and when everyone was sleeping, whether she lie awake or asleep, she continued to hear the cries of dying sheep. Night after night the horrific sounds continued. She would sometimes think of her New Friend and she wished he were there because she would tell him, "This is not music." She tried to imagine other night sounds to replace this 'music.' She imagined crickets, owls, and the sounds of wolves or wildcats. She also imagined the sound of mosquitoes. But nothing in her imagination worked to replace the sound of sheep being murdered.

It turned winter-cold one night and it was on this night she could not sleep at all. She could see that everyone else was peacefully sleeping. Everyone else minus ten. The ten people who had been bathed, linened and led up the hill. None of the ten had returned. She stared up the hill, wondering what took place there. Wondering why no one had returned and why there were no rumors of anyone returning. That's when she made the decision to go to Trophonius on her own. She stood up and as quiet as she had ever been, began walking up the hill. No one was watching. What did she have to lose? She felt guided by this decision, and it was only halfway up the hill that one of the young boys came out of the shadows. She wasn't overly surprised that she was intercepted. She looked down at The Boy and The Boy looked up at her. He was the young one who was excellent with the knife. He was a brown-headed, brown-eyed, brown-skinned, healthy, handsome boy. Even though she didn't have children, she thought he was just young enough that she could be his mother.

She spoke first, "Don't worry, I'll turn around. Can't blame a girl for trying."

The Boy nodded and took it upon himself to escort her back down the hill when he asked, "Isn't that how you get your food, where you are from?"

She asked, "What do you mean?"

The Boy said, "I've seen your face when we kill the sheep."

She said, "Where I come from, it's barbaric."

"Is it?" he asked.

"Yes," she nodded.

"Have you seen how your country raises and slaughters its animals without freedom or love?"

"Yes, I mean no. I understand the system, our system, needs improvement."

"Needs improvement? Who are the barbarians?" he asked.

"Okay maybe we slaughter our livestock very poorly. But the livestock is for us to eat, to live on. You kill to use a sheep's liver to get an answer from God or The Gods?"

"Yes," he said. "But didn't you say you would do anything to get the answer you came for. Isn't that why you are here?"

She couldn't look at him directly. "Yes maybe, in some ways you are right, but what I did not know is that I would be required to take a life to obtain my greatest goal. I think I've made a mistake, I think I want to go home. Do you know when the next bus leaves Trophonius?"

"But didn't you come all this way, to know?"

"Yes."

"You can't turn around now."

"I can. I can do anything I want."

"But you will live to regret it. Imagine how far you've come and then because another culture sacrifices a sheep, you are going to run away. And when you get home, you'll close your eyes and eat your food and you will still not have your answer."

She looked down at him. "You are not a young boy at all, are you? In fact, I think you might be older than I'll ever be. Wiser, for sure." With a maternal instinct that must have been dormant all her life, she touched her hand briefly along the side of his cheek.

He smiled, or was it more of a grin that revealed two of his top front teeth were missing. It was the first time he truly resembled a child. It was the first time he acted his true young age. He said, proudly and shyly, "Thank you."

"Even though you are wiser, I still want to leave. Will you help me leave?"

"There won't be another bus for quite some time."

She remembered the ticket-seller had given her the same line. Quite-some-time must be their stock answer. She proceeded to ask The Boy, "Will you please help me?"

And The Boy answered, "I promise to help you."

CHAPTER TWENTY-THREE

ON THE NEXT SLAYING, the sheep's liver had her name on it. And she didn't blame The Boy, because he was trying to help her in the only way he knew how. He had come to take her down to the Herkyna River. The only thing he told her was to bring her honey-cake.

Down at the ancient river, The Two Boys began to take off her clothes just as she had watched them do to all the others, so mechanically. She would have been uncomfortable with this practice if she weren't depleted by the whole entire thing. From losing Real Love to seeking to know about the future of Real Love; how far she had come and how much further she had to go. She knew beyond knowing that Real Love would not be up in the dark Temple of Fortune because Real Love was the opposite of dark. And yet, perhaps beyond the darkness of Trophonius there would be a connection she hoped. Any kind of connection to Real Love was the only reason she was there.

She allowed The Two Boys to pull her into the river. Where she should have felt anxiety, she instead felt relief. Maybe there was more to a baptism than she had considered before. The Two Boys scrubbed under her two arms and washed her more mildly in other places. The Boy that she knew was shyer than the other one and closed his eyes when her body was standing naked and vulnerable in the clear waters in front of him. The Other Boy, conversely, took all of her in with his eyes. The Boy she knew nudged him to stop looking. And when they dried her, they both looked away. And when wrapping her in white linen their eyes took her in again as she began to take on the appearance of an angel herself. She was filled with hope and light at first and then the dread came on. The dread that could be considered a derivative of fear. She was afraid she had gone too far but she told herself she was not afraid.

The Boy that she knew put his hand on the side of her face, as she had done to him, and said, "All is one." And then he released her and she climbed the hill alone in her white linen shroud, carrying her honey-cake. She trembled as she walked, repeating to herself that she was not afraid.

It was darker at the top than she had expected. Dark, but she could see there were Two Older Boys waiting for her. The Two Older Boys immediately led her through The Temple of Fortune and straight to the altar of Trophonius, which looked similar to all the other antiquated structures of Greece. The stone pillars stood sturdy and were crumbling at the same time. Dozens and dozens of honey-cakes had been left in front of the altar. The Two Older Boys instructed her to bow down and then to leave her own honey-cake as an offering. Her mind went blank, once down on her knees. Leaving her honey-cake at the altar of

Trophonius was the last thing on her mind, and she completed the task without any emotion.

The Two Older Boys then whisked her into a darkness she had never known before. One dark chamber was followed by a glimpse of daylight. Two more dark chambers and then she heard the sound of human sorrow. The sound of humans crying, the sound of humans pleading. She heard but could not see one woman clearly begging, "Please bring me my son back."

Again, she could not see but she could hear the sounds of other women, other families, other humans, speaking, sobbing, begging, wishing and dreaming for whoever was missing in their lives, for their return. No one she heard was pleading for material objects. There was no asking for gold or silver, there was no asking for one pay raise, no promotions, no retirement plans, nothing about a new or an old car. No one asked for property. One hundred percent of what she heard people begging for was only about one thing: missing persons. And yet she could not see exactly where these voices were coming from.

There were more darkened chambers and an occasional flickering of light as she was led to the other side of Trophonius, where there was another group of boys. These boys were digging one small hole with tall ancient tools, similar to farming shovels but much smaller in diameter and much longer in length. She watched them dig with precision and then watched the strongest boy insert a small rickety ladder down into the earth. It was then the group of boys turned toward her because, as it turned out, this was her destination.

The Two Older Boys led her toward the round

hole in the ground. A layer of sweat, at rapid speed, drenched her entire body. The heat and moisture pouring out of her glands was nothing more than fear at the basest level. She found herself frozen with heat, unable to take another step farther. The Two Older Boys locked arms with her and pulled her toward the opening in the earth that had been dug just for her. Without negotiation, they lifted her up and then held her over the gap in the earth. She begged them to stop, to let her go, to let her go back, to let her go home, but they did not answer with words. The Two Older Boys lowered her down into the dark hole. They unlocked their grip, forcing her to climb down the rickety ladder alone.

CHAPTER TWENTY-FOUR

THE ROUND HOLE in the earth was small and compact, an empty cylinder that headed straight down. Her body shook and the ladder shook with her every step downward. Darker than the chambers along the way, darker than her darkest dream, darker than her darkest night, darker than her darkest hour when she lost Real Love. Darker and darker as she climbed down one step at a time. The only thing she could think to do was count the number of steps so that she wouldn't lose her mind, lose her faculties. It was thirty tall steps until she could go no farther. Thirty feet under. She was lower than the dead and buried. Nothing but earth and darkness surrounded her. There was no light above and there was no light below. There was simply no light.

Hyperventilation had already set in and when she gasped for air, the sound of her own breath was amplified. Her breathing, her sobs, her body's convulsions had nowhere to go. The sound of her private agony was deafening, as if she were at the bottom of her own orchestra pit. Any sound she produced blasted louder and at a higher pitch and at a higher vibration. These sound vibrations of her own making reverberated inside her and were not to her liking. She felt immense heat inside and outside her body even though the earth surrounding her was very cold. After a period of time that was impossible to measure, she tried calming herself with inhalations and exhalations, but it hardly worked. She moved to dry her tears, but it was nearly impossible to move her hands and arms upward as there couldn't have been more than a few inches of space surrounding her. When her hands eventually accomplished the task of reaching her eyes, she found her tears had turned into muddy paste—a result caused by the earth's soil in such close proximity.

She spoke aloud for the first time, asking, "Is anyone there?"

There was no response, other than her interior voice telling her quite clearly: *No one is there, no one is expected, you are on your own.*

And then she remembered Aletheia, the Goddess of Truth, and what she told her. *Only one road now, only one story, only now is left.*

She began to weep again, thinking of the beautiful Goddess in all her purity, and then she began to weep even more when thinking of her own personal impurity. Her own personal fate. Had she had gone too far? Yes, she was sure she had. The Valiant Men, The Driver and The Passenger, had warned her. But she hadn't listened. Her weeping turned into cries because of her own personal foolishness. She could blame no one. Only the saddest fool who had ever lived would climb down a dark hole below the living and below the dead. She cried in all configurations of crying:

gentle tears, sobs, outbursts, tears of panic, streams of tears, rivers, until she could cry no more. The dry tears that followed were not unlike the dryness of her last post-alcoholic binge. The dry tears and the dry heaves were somehow related. Her body had finally rejected the sympathy she had created for herself. Her body was through with her despair. Her body was rejecting what she believed she needed. Her body was telling her that crying would do her no good, not anymore. And it was not until all her personal noise stopped that she remembered why she was there.

Real Love. Would he have understood her going this far? He might not have approved, but he would have understood it. Would he have done the same for her, she asked herself? She imagined he wouldn't have had to. He seemed to know more about love than she did. He wouldn't have had to go below the living and the dead to find her. To know. Why did she have to go this far, and what would be the result? Would she die here? If so, and if that meant she would see him, possibly be with him again, would it be worth it? If she died right now, in this very moment, would she then see him again, be with him again?

It was these thoughts that enabled her tears to evaporate. Thinking, asking herself, would she die for him, for Real Love, in this exact moment in order to be with him again? She knew the answer as her breathing was becoming calmer and more natural than it had ever been, other than the calm of when she was by his side. She said it aloud. "Yes."

This was it. She would die here, she would die right now, she would die right in this moment for Real Love. She figured that over time she could not measure, she would eventually suffocate thirty feet below. And indeed Trophonius was dark because The Oracle was the facilitator for people to meet their premature death. She accepted her one road. Fate. She would die here.

And so she waited and she waited and she waited. Without food or drink or light, she waited.

How long she waited, was the question, before she knew she was not going to die there. Without any sign of light, time was impossible to measure. So it was over the longest period of darkness she had ever experienced that she realized her fate was turning out to be worse than death. Because death was either a complete ending, or, as so many people believe death was a transition to a new beginning. If she stayed in this darkness, alive for eternity, it would be worse than permanent death, or worse than any potential transition to any other life. She wanted out. And then she remembered the rickety ladder. She reached for it, but it was gone. She reached upward, but the earth had closed over her.

How long would she be there, what did eternal darkness feel like? Or was this eternal darkness? She thought of all those sad people living above ground, begging for their missing persons to return, asking for their loved ones to come back. At least some people below ground had loved ones waiting for them above. There was no one waiting for her because no one knew she was here. She was alone in a dark hole that she climbed down on her own and the thought of forever was the most exhausting thought that she had ever considered.

It was in looking ahead at her permanent world of

darkness that she thought, what did she possibly have to lose to ask again? If this was it, really it, her one continuous dark empty road in the moment of permanent now, what would she have to lose by asking her truest question again? She had risked everything for this. She had, for all intents and purposes, given away her entire soul for this one question. She spoke aloud.

"Trophonius, are you there? You must be. How else would I end up here if it weren't for you?"

She received no answer from the darkness.

"So Trophonius, will I ever see him again? Real Love? Is he in darkness, too? Where is he exactly? Where is my one and only love? Is he okay? I would be more peaceful if I knew he were okay. Even if I weren't able to see him again. Just to know he's okay would bring my world of darkness some light."

Nothing from Trophonius, nothing from the darkness.

"I want to know," she demanded.

More nothingness came from Trophonius. During this vast silence, she tried to bring up images of Real Love in her head. She could come up with nothing. She couldn't conjure up an image of one happy moment or simply one image of him. She tried imagining him, remembering him in their apartment, but he was not there. In his office or on the street, but he was not there. He was not anywhere she would typically visualize him. Nothing was coming up. Not an image of his face, no image of his hands, not his naked body, not any part of his flesh. Nothing. Would darkness deprive her of that too, of the memory of Real Love? She had to accept the darkness but she did not have to accept the loss of memory of Real Love. She would not permit it.

"You will not take him away from me, Trophonius; you are not more powerful than I am. I will remember him and I will remember him now."

And she did. But it was not a memory she wanted. It was his last hour. It was the hour she had willingly blocked, the one she had chosen not to see again, the one she had chosen not to remember. She had built a fortress around this hour and now the fortress was gone.

It had been the most beautiful day ever. It was spectacular sun and a spectacular breeze. The type of morning when everything is possible.

It was that feeling of possibility on the sailboat that day. Friends of theirs had a boat and would often sail on the Hudson River. It had been one of those days when they could have spent the entirety of it in bed, with the breeze coming through their window. Yet they forced themselves to stop lovemaking to go and spend the day with their friends, and they were jointly happy with this decision.

The first hour on the Hudson River was perfect, but then the storm came. The boat had sailed too far past the Verrazano Narrows Bridge where the Hudson meets the Atlantic Ocean. And the irony was, they all survived the lightening and thunderstorm. When the storm cleared they could see theirs was the only boat that was still out too far. All the other boats had made it safely back to the various docks and harbors—theirs was the only boat in sight. Once they put up the sails again, while the sun lit up the sky again, it was a celebration because nothing disastrous had happened. Everyone on the boat, including the nondrinkers, took a sip from the lukewarm champagne bottle that was passed around, and some of the happy survivors danced to the static coming from the radio. Until one of the guests, a woman that nobody knew well, a woman who had come with a friend of a friend of a friend, fell overboard and disappeared into the ocean's depths. That was the beginning of their end.

He, Real Love, dove straight into the ocean after the woman nobody knew well to help her. He dove under several times, coming up for air again and again. He was unable to find her. Until he found her. He, with all his strength, pulled her towards the boat and the group of friends onboard pulled her up. The woman was fine and it was a real life victory. And she was proud of him, her Real Love. Sunlight reflected a billion tiny ocean mirrors surrounding him. Their eyes locked, she above and he below, the intensity of their bond was magnified by the power of the ocean's waves and glistening waters. And then a blink or was it a flash later, he disappeared. The bright, glistening water engulfed him and he was gone.

Other friends, other men, jumped in to help him. She didn't panic at first because she knew he'd be fine just as the woman nobody knew well turned out to be fine. And then all the other men with all their diving under and coming back up for air couldn't find him. Her friends voices kept repeating, the current was too strong. The current's never been so strong. She dove in after him and it was true. The current was too strong and he was not strong enough.

She had recalled his image all right. She had defied Trophonius because she was able to recall Real Love in her mind. But that was all she could recall: his diving in, his saving another's life, and then a flash and then his being pulled under to his death.

Again she saw it: he dives in, he saves another's life, a flash, he drowns. Repeat after repeat.

That was all she could see in her permanent sea of darkness. Real Love dying over and over again. How long these images replayed, she didn't know. If the sun created a billion ocean mirrors that day, could she replay his death a billion times? Eternity surely went on past the billions. At first it was exhausting imaging his death over and over again, and then it became rather ordinary. It numbed the mind as well as the heart. He dives, he saves, a flash, he drowns. And what of the blink or the flash before he was pulled under? What did it mean, if anything? Was it the sun or the mind playing tricks or did the spark of light have any meaning? He dives, he saves, a flash, he's gone.

Her mind then skipped to the hours later, when the Coast Guard pulled his body out of the water with ropes and netting. There was no flash or blink, it was a dull experience that held no adrenaline. The Coast Guard had come to find him. His body lay there on the deck, drenched and dead. There was no potential revival, no heroic tale to tell. It was death right in front of her. The death of the most real thing she ever had experienced. The death of her soul companion, the death of not only Real Love but the death of the person who taught her that love was indeed possible. That love existed.

The one thing that was exceedingly clear to her when his dead body was exposed and laid out, and when a man in uniform manually pumped the water out of his body, was that he was not there anymore. The look on her friends' faces was that of being frightened, and yet she was, in fact, not afraid. She knew he wasn't there. His spirit had gone, but where had it gone? Yes, she felt his presence still, but it was not coming from his dead, cold body stretched out in front of her. Hands and arms tried to pull her away from him. She held his hand knowing he was not there anymore until the Man in Uniform detached her hand and then covered his body. It seemed permanent, but it didn't feel permanent.

Where did he go, she wondered from that very moment until now? She wanted to know where he went. If she felt his presence and if that were the truth, he could not have met his permanent death. And so where was he? Strangely, she believed he was okay, but she did not know it for a fact. There was no frantic intuition that he was being harmed or in an underground hole permanently filled with darkness. She knew otherwise, but what did she really know? Nothing. Nothing at all except the feeling that she believed she would see him again. How or where or why or when was not what she wanted to know. She just wanted the absolute certainty that she would see him again. She did not have an agenda or an inkling of an idea of what it would be like. It was far too mysterious for her to grasp.

All she wanted to know was to know. In this dark, deep hole under the dead and under the living, she was still yearning beyond yearning to know.

And no one thus far, not one human being she had known, not one stranger along the way, not even a Priestess, not a Goddess, not a Philosopher had been able to give her the answer. And what about Aristotle? Nobody except The Tourist in New York seemed to know anything about him.

Her mind's recollection was now seeing his body being pulled out of the water, his body lying on the deck and the Uniformed Man pumping water from his body, and the Uniformed Man pulling her hand from his hand. Her mind recalled every single frame as the memory-record replayed itself: his body was there, his spirit was no longer living in his body, yet his spirit seemed to be living somewhere.

He had saved someone's life. Would she have traded the woman he saved to have her Real Love back? She could not even tempt herself to attempt an answer. Would she have given away the life of a friend of a friend of a friend to drown in the ocean to have her Real Love back? Again, she averted her mind from the question.

He had chosen this. He had chosen to give his life for another. Would she have done the same at the risk of losing him? She didn't think she would. In fact, she had done the reverse—she had taken a life, the life of an animal, a poor sheep, to enhance her own.

Real Love had given a life to someone, she had taken a life. He was better than she and she knew it. She hated this fact, especially in the darkness. She could not escape the sobering fact that he was a better man than she was a woman, and the fact that he saved a life and she had killed one. The sound of the murdered sheep returned. And she decided that the best thing she could do was to try and forget all about love in any form. If he came back right now, he would be the hero and she would be the villain. He had lived the better life. Does living longer make you better, she asked herself? No, living a long life gives a human more opportunity for failure. She had surpassed failure. In fact, she had exposed herself so greatly that she was living under the earth in permanent darkness.

The best and only thing she could do for herself was to try not to think of him again. And so she didn't. She put Real Love far away from her thoughts and feelings. The thought of The Priestess under the Oak Tree returned to her but she rejected it. And she did not want to think of The Goddess either, or anyone good that she had met. She did not offer thankfulness for one thing. Instead she focused on the darkness, the darkness that she had manifested and would live with forever. At that moment she was comfortable with her decision. Because once anyone gets used to such great darkness, it's the most comfortable place to be. It lacks mystery and there is no lower place to go. She therefore concluded there was no other destination for her other than the permanent loss of all hopes or feelings.

Her aspirations for anything had gone away, and so she decided to offer gratefulness for one last entity, "Praise to the Oracle of Trophonius for bringing me here."

She wanted nothing more than to be completely withdrawn from any human memory. It didn't matter whether her eyes were open or closed because darkness begets darkness, darkness equals darkness. And there was no rest from this profound darkness, there was no sleep, there was simply utter darkness.

CHAPTER TWENTY-FIVE

LEGENDS SAY that whenever a child is born feet first, he or she is a healer. And so when her feet ascended from the oracular underground first, she figured the legend must not be true. She was no healer. She didn't know who or what she was. She didn't even know why or how she remembered such a legend. The gentle pull from above enabled her to rise effortlessly from the earth. A Group of Boys assisted her. She not only didn't know who the Group of Boys were, she had not the vaguest notion of where she was or how she had come to be there.

Without recollection of much, she allowed The Boys to escort her down a valley toward an old fashioned throne where a Panel of Priest-Scholars, of all varieties of age, sat in a semi-circle with wooden tablets and wooden writing instruments. The Boys told her she had arrived at the Throne of Memory and left her there.

A Middle-Aged Man, or perhaps he was a Patient, was being interviewed by The Panel of Priest-Scholars. She was too far away to hear what was being said. The

Patient seemed frustrated while the Priest-Scholars were taking notes. Later, when The Patient was being escorted away, the only thing she could hear was the sound of the man's voice babbling nonsense.

Intuitively, she stood up to take her turn. She walked to the front of the Throne of Memory where she took a seat in a regal, uncomfortable chair made of stone. The youngest, the Junior Priest-Scholar began her session by asking what she remembered since being at the Oracle of Trophonius.

She responded by telling him, "Nothing."

The Junior Scholar then asked, "Do you remember arriving at Trophonius?"

"What's Trophonius?" And before he could answer, she had already asked him another question, "What kind of priests are you all?"

The Junior Scholar answered, "We ask the questions, you answer them."

She responded, "But aren't you supposed to help me?" when she realized that one of The Panelists was transcribing her every word onto a wooden tablet.

The Junior Scholar was kind when he asked again, "Please, for your own benefit, what is your last memory?"

"Being pulled from the earth against my will."

"And before that?"

"Nothing. Empty blank dark nothing."

"And before that?"

"Nothing."

"Do you remember where you were born?"

"In a hospital, of course."

"Do you remember in what region you were born, or what region you have come from?"

She did not answer because she did not know.

"Do you remember your parents, or did you have parents at all?"

She labored over the question before answering, "I believe I must have had parents, it would be logical that I did, but I have no memory of them."

"What is logical?" he asked.

But she could not answer.

The Panel Transcriptionist continued carving her every word and reaction onto his wooden tablet.

"Do you have children?"

"I don't believe I do."

"Do you have a husband?"

"I don't believe so."

"Who is your truest friend, or do you have one?"

"I don't know."

"Do you remember anything about a family member, or a friend? Or any one person?"

It was then she began to babble just as the Middle-Aged Patient had done. She didn't know what she was saying and worse, she didn't know what she was trying to articulate. These were mismatched words that had no rhyme or reason. The Panel Transcriptionist wrote down her every word: "Chalk board, partly cloudy, tea not coffee, gas tank, Philadelphia, rulers and yard sticks, never cut flowers." And though her list of non-sequitur words went on and on, the Transcriptionist was able to keep up with her, recording her every utterance.

"How do you feel?" the Junior Scholar asked.

"What is it to feel?"

"Are you hot or cold?"

"I don't know."

"Do you feel any emotion?"

"I already told you, I don't feel."

"Do you have emotion?"

"I don't know what that is."

The Junior Scholar did not ask another question, instead, he waited for her to begin babbling again.

She countered by asking him another question, filled with composure, "Do I go back now?"

"Where is back?"

"Down into the cylinder of darkness."

"No, you will not being going back there."

With the blankest of expressions, she asked, "Where will I go?"

"That's up to you."

Her hand involuntarily went to scratch the top of her forehead, which had the same texture of the stone on the regal chair she was seated on, rough and immoveable. Her non-sequitur speech patterns started up again. "Lack of sun, fat-free milk, silkscreen, down a pancake, jogging, spoke not a wheel, overture, never cut flowers."

And as with the Middle-Aged Patient, she was escorted down from the Throne of Memory and taken to an open-air community where other lost souls were supervised. Most individuals at the Community of Lost Souls more or less kept to themselves—they took circular walks, they ate and drank together but never commiserated. They slept on cots outdoors and were monitored round the clock, although there were no clocks.

When her peers were sleeping, she stared up at the bright lights shining down on them all with fascination. She did not remember the name of the bright lights shining from above, but a sensation stirred inside her. She wondered if this was relevant to the emotion the Junior Scholar had inquired about.

When she returned to the Throne of Memory, she tried to describe what was up above, the glittering lights that shined when it was dark, but she was unable to name what she saw. She figured she must have seen those lights before and so asked The Panel, "What are the bright lights that come from above, what are they called, and where do they come from?"

The Junior Scholar did not answer her, rather he asked, "When or where did you learn the following words: Bright lights, glittering, shining down and up above. What do these words mean to you?"

"They do not mean anything to me, I was only curious."

"And you felt no emotion?"

"A stirring, perhaps."

"That is the beginning of emotion."

"Is emotion good or bad?"

"Why does something have to be good or bad?"

"I don't know."

The Panelists discussed this between themselves. And then the Eldest Panelist asked, "Where did you acquire the basic concept of only good or only bad?"

She didn't know but decided to guess her answer, "Perhaps I learned this in my region, my country."

"And what country is that?"

"North America."

The entire group of Panelists inscribed this onto their tablets. The Eldest Panelist then asked another question, "What is the difference between illusion and reality, or is there one?"

"Hydrates and carbohydrates, television, warfare and lovefare, thanklessness, sun dried tomatoes, never cut flowers," was all she said.

She did not know how many times she was taken to the Throne of Memory because she no longer knew how to count, but she did hold the memory that at one time, she did not know when or how, she did know how to count. She probed her mind, asking herself under the flickering lights that lit up the darkness above, why she could remember some things and not others. She wondered what was holding her back from memory, but she did not share this with The Panelists. She had decided her private thoughts should be kept to herself. The only thing she knew at this point was that she did not want to keep going back to the Throne of Memory for the rest of her life. When her mind spoke the word *life* to itself, another wave of stirrings moved across her chest. *Life*, she wondered, why did that word propel her into thinking deeper? Probing deeper. Why did sensation move across her chest and would she ask The Panelists such a question? She didn't want to be judged or used as a scientific experiment. Most interior thoughts she reminded herself were best kept to herself. If she kept everything inside, no harm could reach her.

She never spoke to the Middle-Aged Patient nor did he speak to her, but she did watch him being escorted down the opposite side of the valley, where she witnessed a cluster of people waiting for him. He stepped into the cluster that included a woman his age, children and elders. Perhaps this was a family. His family.

Her chest tightened on the thought of family.

She tried to remember something about family, but she could not remember a thing. It therefore registered that when she was released, if ever she were released, that probably no one would be waiting for her. If she couldn't remember a loved one, she concluded he would not remember her either. He. Her mind had chosen the word he. The tightness around her chest became softer, outlining an oval sac within her chest. Involuntarily, she recalled the word pericardium. She did not recall what the word meant. A circular energy moved around this pericardium area, whatever it was. It was uncomfortable in its strangeness. If this is what it is to feel, she thought, she did not want to feel a thing.

Over the course of time that she could not measure, she witnessed more peers from the Community of Lost Souls reuniting with their families at the bottom of the valley. Since she did not wish to feel a thing, she would turn her back on such reunions. Therefore, no sensations positive or negative erupted. And the more sessions with The Panelists that came and went, the more she learned to control her babbling in front of them. Whenever her mind recalled words such as blood and sheep killings and hopelessness and lovelessness, she did not tell The Panelists. Instead, she chose the in-between words that comprised part of her thinking pattern but were not the driving force behind her thoughts. She offered them words such as: air, grass and rivers. It was involuntarily that all her non-sequiturs ended with the words: never cut flowers. And although it was unspoken, she knew that they knew she was intentionally not sharing her insanity with them. She had trained her mind not to offer them a shred of insight into her interior world.

She continued to fight memory and emotion, while her pericardium continued to circulate energy. Sometimes the movement outlining her pericardium traveled clockwise and other times it traveled counter-clockwise. The thing that irritated her most about the whole thing was that the lining of her pericardium never went dormant, and so it forced her to feel. Most bewilderingly, the feelings the pericardium stirred up were never-ending, not even during sleeping hours. Sleeping and wakefulness were hardly different. These unwanted feelings made her long for the dark cylinder where she could escape. Underground, there had been no word recollections, there had been no emotion. Pericardiums had not existed.

She saw a Long-Legged Man she recognized but didn't know from where she recognized him. Neither of them ever looked directly at the other; she observed him whenever he was not looking. Perhaps he did the same with her, but it didn't matter to her in the slightest. What did matter was his behavior. He, like her, had abnormal sleeping patterns and also did not give away his inner thoughts to The Panel of Priest-Scholars. He, too, had learned to control his babbling, and on many nights, she watched him murmuring into his pillow. She learned this from him and so whenever she felt a wave of nonsense coming on, she would lie face down and ramble non-sequiturs into her bedding: hopscotch, post office, atlas, high dive, litter, wing, song. And although she tried not to say it, again she repeated the refrain of never cut flowers.

The familiar faces from the Community of Lost Souls had mostly gone. Brand new Lost Souls emerged from the darkness almost daily. Perhaps she recognized the Long-Legged Man by virtue of the fact that they had been there the longest without being released. Senior inmates, she thought. Silent allies.

More and more Lost Souls reunited with their families. Each and every time, she turned her back so as to not see them. If she did not see the families, they did not exist. But the problem was that her mind's awareness was heightened even without the gift of sight. Her mind knew that endless streams of families were coming to take their loved ones home. Every time her mind thought of the idea of family, whether a brief or a lingering thought, her pericardium activated more fully, which triggered a warming sensation inside of her. A depth of emotion she did not desire. And whenever her mind lingered on the word family, and it was always against her will, it reminded her again and again that it was unlikely any family would be waiting for her and that he would not be waiting for her. *He* had come up again. Her mind was selecting the word *he*.

There were no reunions at night, and yet it was at nighttime that flashbacks of the word he would recur. *He.* Her mind struggled, wondering who he was. The warmth emitting from the center of her pericardium began to travel throughout her entire body, from the tips of her fingers to the tips of her toes. What was this heat inside of her, she asked herself, where did it come from? Nighttime and darkness surrounded her. She stared up at the flickering lights that lit up the above and contemplated who *he* might be. *He.* It was without focusing on the flickering lights that she remembered their names. "Stars," she whispered aloud. Suddenly, an overwhelming sense of emotion swept through her body.

On the remembrance of what stars were and on

her curiosity surrounding the word *he*, she decided on this particular moonless night she would not battle the gentle warmth circulating inside her body. Instead she would allow herself to try to experience the strange sensation of feeling. She would not have to tell anyone about it, she could keep it to herself. She tried relaxing, exploring the notion of emotion as raw and peculiar as it was. She closed her eyes, joining the Community of Lost Souls under the stars where they would dream their dreams together.

CHAPTER TWENTY-SIX

HER NIGHTTIME VISION was not what she wanted it to be. It was not dull or numb the way she had trained it to be. Her nighttime vision had begun to navigate on its own.

She began to see moving pictures of her life, the one she hadn't remembered: she saw her two parents on the day she was born, she saw herself as a child taking her first few steps before falling, she saw herself wearing her first dress, riding her first bike. It was as if she were watching an old movie of herself, one she could not interact with. She could not reach out to touch her parents or herself. She could not reach out to change a thing. These were all vivid images of the positive nature. She saw herself driving a car for the first time, she saw herself graduating high school, she saw herself terrified on the high dive but diving in anyway. She saw herself studying for college finals, she saw her first job interview, she saw her first day at the office. And then she saw him.

There he was. The mysterious *he* was no longer an unknown. He was standing right in front of her, fully imaged. All happy memories, a beautiful perfect film, everything was good in his world. Their world. The first day they met, their first walk together, their first disagreement, their first resolution. She tried to reach out and touch him but was unable to do so, and then she reminded herself she would not change a thing. The first time they made love, and every time they made love until the last time they made love. Their perfect momentary world of love, truth, sex, adoration, and the learning and relearning of selflessness, giving and receiving. Superseding all this was trust. And playfulness of the joyous kind. Love. So much of it, to be given away. Their perfect world played like the best movie there ever was, in black and white. *To Have and to Have Not*, in which Harry Steve Morgan and Marie Slim Browning would meet for the first time and they would leave Martinique together and they would live forever.

But theirs was a different ending. The sound of the ocean's waves altered her night vision from the flickering light of the stars above, back to the darkness of Trophonius.

The moving pictures she began to experience were: he dives into the ocean, he saves another's life, and then in a flash, he is pulled underwater. And repeat: he dives in, he saves another's life, a flash, he drowns. As if back underground at Trophonius, her memory replayed him. Real Love, dying over and over again until she woke up amongst her fellows, the Community of Lost Souls.

She looked at all the other Lost Souls who were still dreaming. She did not want to stay there at the Throne of Memory, endlessly watching everyone else getting their memories back, watching everyone else getting healed, watching everyone else getting released, watching everyone else reuniting with their families who were still alive.

But she did not want to be released where love no longer existed. She wanted to return to the dark cylinder of Trophonius.

She stood up and began walking back towards the hill. It was not the moon but the stars that guided her back to Trophonius. She searched for and found The Temple of Fortune, she passed the hundreds of honey-cakes at the altar, and she found the exact same passage she had taken before. She passed through all the chambers that she had gone through before, darker and darker with intermittent flickerings of light. She heard the sound of human sorrow like she had before, but this time, she thought she could hear the sound of her own sorrowful voice in the choir of sadness. She continued through all the darkest chambers and not one soul followed her. Her memory had returned so perfectly that she soon found the very hole in the ground that had been dug just for her.

Her personal cylinder of darkness had been closed and covered up with a layer of fresh dirt. And so she fell down onto her knees and with her bare hands began to uncover her personal underground cylinder. Soon her hands were filthy and soon, she thought, she would descend down to where there was no memory and there were no pericardiums and there was no love and moreover, there was no loss of love.

It was before she was able to fully uncover the hole when she heard a woman's voice shouting from the underground, "Back off!"

She looked down into the earth but could not see the Woman Underground. She spoke down to the voice, "What are you doing in my cylinder?"

The Woman Underground replied, "It is not your cylinder anymore. Now go away."

"No, this dark hole is mine. I watched a group of boys dig it specifically for me."

"I've waited five years for this moment with Trophonius and you're ruining it. You've had your turn, now leave."

"But I don't like it up here, I want to return to Trophonius."

"You had your chance, now this is my chance, please go away," the Woman Underground begged her.

"But where will I go?"

"What do I care, I'm down here in my own sorrow. If I am this low, how can I help you? You are on a higher rung than I am."

"I don't feel higher."

"But you feel. Leave me alone, please. I've lost my only son and all I want is to know that he's okay."

"I believe your son is okay, everybody's okay *after.*"

"Yes, but do you know it? All I want is to know. That's why I am here."

She understood how the Woman Underground felt and so she re-covered the cylinder with all the loose dirt and while doing so she heard the sound of the woman weeping for her lost son until she couldn't weep anymore. And then she heard the Woman Underground begging the Oracle of Trophonius, "I want to know, I need to know." And the more she heard the Woman Underground repeating herself, she felt as if she were listening to the sound of her own voice.

She was looking across the peaks and valleys of Trophonius that were strangely beautiful and peaceful when she caught the sight of a tall ancient shovel, which the Group of Boys must have left behind.

It was with this ancient tool she began to dig her own underground cylinder of darkness. It was much more difficult than she thought; the Group of Older Boys who had dug such holes were much stronger than they looked. She wondered if everyone did everyone else's job at one time or another, however brief, perhaps misunderstandings would turn out to be understandings. She was relieved when The Two Older Boys she had met before approached her because she thought they had come to help, but, in fact they strongly suggested that she leave. It was explained that if she left of her own free will, it would be best because the forms of retribution for breaking rules at Trophonius were the opposite of pleasant.

Against her instincts, she manifested her will to escort herself back to the Community of Lost Souls. Along the path she had been on before, she saw the familiar group of Young Boys swimming in the river. She watched The Young Boys taking turns diving from a cliff into the deepest part of the water. They swam like innocent children. An outside observer would not have an inkling these boys could slaughter a sheep without flinching. And she had little emotion while watching them. The splashing of the water turned stillness into waves, turning one reflection into a million reflections, glistening, and a billion mirrors later and one single flash caused her to consider her life's options.

She waited until The Young Boys exhausted themselves and left for the day. She waited until dusk before she headed down to the river on her own. Along the way, along the path she had never been on before, she picked up the largest stones she could find and carried them inside the fabric of her white linen shroud.

It was twilight when she stood at the riverbank wondering why she hadn't considered this option before. She looked into the river's water and recalled one thing: a flash and he's gone.

She was not ungrateful for her life. In fact, she remembered The Priestess under the Oak Tree and decided to recount everything that had happened to her in thankfulness before she, too, would be gone. She spent her last moments giving thanks for every single thing that had happened to her. She thanked God or The Gods or The Goddess or The Goddesses for him. For Real Love. And then she thanked all these Deities for the mind and the wisdom for choice and for ending her life there in the perfection of Trophonius. She stepped into the water with the largest stones she could carry. She insisted to herself that she still was not bold, but she was not afraid.

She stood knee-deep in the river and it was one of the most divine moments of her life. She did not want a thing more from life; she was ready to say goodbye. She stepped farther and farther, until the river reached her shoulders. She smiled at how magnificent life really was and how wondrous to have choices at every turn. "There is only one story, one road now. Only now is left." And she listened to the sounds, the sound of the river, the sound of night falling, the day creatures saying goodbye and the night creatures greeting her hello, the sound of her breathing. Her New Friend had been right, "Music is the key to everything."

And then she sang, "All I want is to know."

She walked farther underwater, where she was no longer visible from above. She held the stones across her pericardium so that she would not rise to the top, and when she relaxed, she was able to lie down at the bottom of the riverbed. Her eyes remained open observing everything she could until the very end. Colorful fish swam above her and one black snake circled so close it brushed her hand. Her breathing drank in the water, and she did not fight it. She began to choke, but she embraced the feeling of leaving. She embraced the feeling of what it would be to know.

CHAPTER TWENTY-SEVEN

IT WAS A PRESENCE that brought her to shore and laid her down on the riverbank. It did not seem to be a human form and she assumed she would never know. Whatever it was, whoever it was, that pulled her out of the river was no longer present. She was alone, coughing and breathing life back into her lungs when she heard a boy's voice, "You can't step in the same river twice."

She saw that it was The Young Boy with the two missing front teeth. The Boy continued, "For other waters are constantly flowing in."

"Don't tell me you're a philosopher too?" she asked while gasping for air.

"No, I learned about rivers and poetry in school. Some math also, but I don't like numbers. Heraclitus also said, 'The only thing constant is constant change.'"

Heraclitus, she pondered, but didn't bother telling him she didn't have a clue as to who Heraclitus was. She asked, "So since you are such a smart kid, I suppose you're the one who pulled me out of the river without my permission?"

"Nope," he replied.

"Did you see who did?"

"Negative."

"I don't think it's right that someone or something interfered with my plan to leave my life behind."

"You mean suicide? The Boy asked.

She thought suicide was a big word for a small boy.

"The content of your character is your choice. Day by day, what you do is who you become." The Boy said.

"And yet, I don't want to be here anymore."

"Don't you?"

She couldn't answer him honestly, not out loud anyway. It was a weak choice to want to end her life without knowing. They both knew that. It was something they didn't need to discuss.

He added, "Integrity is your destiny. It is the light that guides your way."

"Okay then. But I don't want to go back to Trophonius or that Throne of Memory. Please don't make me go back. Didn't you promise that you would help me? What do the philosophers say about promises?"

"I haven't been educated about promises yet. Maybe that comes later?"

She giggled with The Boy as if they were the same young age. This caused the side of her face to hurt. Her facial muscles and skin hadn't moved since sitting on the regal chair at the Throne of Memory. Or perhaps her facial expressions hadn't been activated since descending into the oracular cylinder of the underground. Her absence of emotion had kept her face at a degree below frozen and it took over a thousand invisible needles prickling across her face for it to begin to unthaw.

She did not tell The Boy about the pain she was experiencing for she knew it was temporary. Rather, she asked him the simplest of questions, "I don't suppose you know anything about Aristotle?"

He didn't answer because he didn't know and she didn't press him on the subject because no one, thus far, had known.

She then asked, "So, are you going to help me this time?"

"I could get in trouble," he said.

"I'm in trouble, I've gone too far. If you were to get lost and you didn't even know where you were, wouldn't you want someone or something to come along and help get you out of it?"

"Not if the someone or something helping me was going to get in trouble."

"I understand," was all she could think to say.

"There are secret tunnels that connect the Oracle of Trophonius to the Oracle of Delphi."

"I don't wish to go to another Oracle. None of them have helped me. I wish to return. I'm ready to return."

"Return where?"

"Where I came from."

"There may be an exit you can take inside one of the tunnels."

"There may be? I don't want a may-be. I want to get out of here."

"If you choose any other road above ground, you will be seen."

She looked around the deceptively tranquil setting of Trophonius with the quaint town below, and the small chapel above reflecting light. She took it all in with her eyes one last time—the wild animals and the wildflowers, no fences—and then she allowed The Boy to guide her to the secret tunnels.

They traveled by foot across the river and into emerald fields that had never seen the likes of a lawnmower. There was uncut grass that was taller than The Boy, and more grass that followed was even taller than her, with green blossoms and flowers sprouting from almost every blade. Illuminated by the sun, the uncut grass was yet another symphony of wildlife and the wind orchestrated the dancing grass to sing. Music was the key to everything, she thought quietly to herself, as any spoken word would certainly ruin the tribute of the moment.

The Boy led her to the front of a dark tunnel surrounded by the wildest roses she had ever seen. The most brilliant colors, predominantly shades of red, climbed up and over the tunnel's entrance as if the roses believed they were a never-ending vine. Unmanicured buds, blossoms, branches and leaves that had probably, like the grass, never been near anything that resembled a gardening sheer.

The Boy broke the silence when he told her not to be afraid and not to judge what she would find inside the tunnels.

"Will there be more darkness?" she asked.

"The way up and the way down are one in the same. What was scattered, gathers."

"More Heraclitus?" she asked.

He nodded and then offered her one last thought, "Only change is real."

She leaned down to hug The Boy as if he were

her own. She was surprised that his return embrace was equal to hers — as if they belonged together, mother and son or son and mother, and that when they parted, they would no longer belong together. She also knew the feeling of wanting to hold onto something forever and that that was clearly an impossibility. Love and change were the only two real things she had ever known. And all that was left for her now was change. Strange that it would be a young boy who would teach her that. They let go of each other's embrace at the same time. She waited for him to reveal his two missing teeth one last time before she went inside the tunnel.

CHAPTER TWENTY-EIGHT

THE BOY HAD led her appropriately—there was no more darkness. The tunnels with dirt roads had giant candles burning upon elaborate candelabrums at every turn. There were artistic carvings and sculptures cut into the clay walls but she did not stop to consider their significance. She put one foot in front of the other at a steady pace. She saw a few others, young women and young men in uniforms of soft burlap, walking more briskly than herself, and in both directions. Their voices never rose above a whisper. They were not soldiers; they looked more to be religious acolytes. Whether Trophoniuns or Delphites, she didn't really care. For all she knew, they could have been followers of Heraclitus. No matter, she walked as if she knew where she was going and therefore no one stopped her or asked her who she was or where she was going. And no one in fact greeted her; she felt unseen.

Only one road now, she thought, her one road to change. She hadn't come all this way to let the love of her life go, she had come to know that she would somehow, some way see him again. All she had wanted was to know. And what she knew in this new moment of perpetual change was that she was not going to get the answer that she had come for. With each step forward, she tried with everything left inside of her to cope with the fact that her one road was a complete unknown. A road without Real Love. Except for memories of Real Love. And who wants to spend the rest of their life living in a memory? Not her. She would shake this off someday. She didn't know how she would do it. All she could do was try.

It was not a direct route—there were so many twists and turns and seemingly u-turns, she did not know which direction she was headed but she felt she was on the right path. It was not until she came across a spattering of natural daylight that she felt an actual sense of hope. Her hope was no longer to know if she would see him again. Her hope was solely focused on returning.

The outdoor light brightened the tunnel's dirt floor, reaching her bare feet. She looked out into the blinding daylight and appreciated the sheer warmth from the rays of sun. Instinctively she moved towards the light, the intensity of which forced her eyes to narrow and she could not see what was past the entrance, or exit, as it were. She moved toward and through the light, and she walked straight into a man's arms, bumping him, almost knocking him over.

The man impatiently waited for her to move around him. She told him she was sorry, that she couldn't see as she came into the light. He didn't respond, as he was too busy juggling writing notes with his right hand while holding onto a notepad and a glass jar containing a small insect with his left hand.

He more or less ignored her, making her feel unseen, as did all the others in the tunnel she had passed.

He looked different than the others, no uniform, though dressed in a formal dark suit that seemed to be designed especially for him. Unlike all the Trophoniuns and Delphites, he was clean cut and rather gorgeous for a man. He seemed to know he was gorgeous, which gives a man an entirely different disposition than the man who is unknowingly so. The man was fortified with himself. Attractive indeed, and even though he hadn't spoken a word to her, his charisma was startling. She hadn't felt a real sense of attraction to any man since Real Love, and so she thought it was a sign of the change she was not ready to admit to and she continued past him out into the daylight.

Once outside, the man asked, "Why have you come here?"

"I came here in search of an answer, but unfortunately, I received an answer I didn't want."

"Well dear, you've come to the most archaic place for any answer, or any question for that matter."

"What are you doing here if this place is so archaic?"

"Observing the men and women sneaking in and out of these tunnels, trading information from one supposed Oracle to the next. All trickery instead of truth. You see?"

He pointed her vision toward a gathering of more young people in uniform: All were exchanging notes and ideas between the two colonies of Trophonius and Delphi.

"Oracles!" he said. "All absolutely made up for one thing and one thing only. Money. Deceiving your fellow human to make money: preposterous!"

Her heart sank. Had everything thus far been a hoax? She wondered, were Oracles nothing more than myths? She chose not to respond to the man, instead, she watched him continue to handwrite copious notes with his right hand and continue to juggle his notepad and the glass jar with his left. Inside the jar, she could see the lone insect with wings was attempting to fly.

She asked, "Why are you holding a firefly hostage inside a glass jar?"

"Everyone knows I collect specimens. I was about to take this one inside the darkened tunnel to see if he or she would illuminate during the day, giving the specimen the pretenses that it is night."

"Even if you put every single firefly into complete darkness during the day, not one of them will light up because they all know it is not nighttime."

"How do they know it is not nighttime?"

"I don't know how, all I can tell you is they just know."

"They just know? That concept holds no logic. How did you come across your claim to knowing this?"

"We all caught lightening bugs and fireflies when we were children. None of them light up during the day, not even in total darkness. They only light up at night. It's a fact."

"And what else do you claim to know about fireflies?"

"They don't live very long."

"Does any thing or any being live as long as they desire?"

"And they light up every few seconds to attract their mates. The masculine light is stronger than the feminine light. And once the male firefly finds his female firefly, their light starts to blink in unison."

"And then," he concluded for her, "They make love."

"Love?"

"Love is a single soul inhabiting two bodies."

She had heard that the Mediterraneans had particular womanizing skills, but hadn't encountered it so closely. It was definitely time for her to return home. She decided the best thing to do was to not respond.

"And why, dear, did you really come to Greece? Yes, you received the answer you didn't want. Was there any other mission you wished to achieve before returning? Were you not looking for a specific someone?"

She admitted, "True, I had been searching for any information I could find about Aristotle. But I've given up on that, too."

"And what if you've finally found him?" he offered.

"Aristotle?" she laughed, "That can't be true."

"Whether true or not, can't we make it true?"

Again she didn't answer; she looked in another direction far, far away.

With both his hands, he turned her face back in his direction before he asked, "What did you want with Aristotle, anyway?"

She hesitated at first, and then said, "All women by nature desire to know."

CHAPTER TWENTY-NINE

THE MAN WHO called himself Aristotle brought her coffee in bed. She knew he wasn't Aristotle and she knew she could have resisted him, but she figured on her new one road of perpetual change, she ought to at least try to participate in human behavior, primitive as it was. What she didn't expect was that he would make love to her as if she were a scientific experiment. Anytime she felt pleasure, the moment after, he would write a long-drawn-out summary into his journal. Or anytime she would sexually-drift, he would inquire as to what had gone wrong. And even though she didn't like to speak about sex the way so many women do, he forced her to describe what pleased her and moreover what did not please her. Everything she had to say, he wrote down with glee, converse to the countless times with men before Real Love who never really listened. He was an avid listener and lecturer in one. And even though he took himself so seriously, he also wielded a marked sense of humor. What's more, he made her skin feel young again.

It was during one of their breaks from lovemaking,

when everything was silent and when she thought he had fallen asleep, that she noticed the captured firefly was alighting inside the glass jar. She watched the insect struggling to be free until the need for action overcame her. She tiptoed over to the glass jar, took off the lid and released the lightening bug out the window. She watched the grateful insect fly out into the night. When she turned around, the man who called himself Aristotle was standing right behind her. He didn't scold, instead he whispered to her, "Nature does nothing uselessly."

They looked out the window together, observing bands of fireflies blinking their way across the landscape. As they watched, he quietly said, "Some animals are social. They like to hang out in groups, such as fireflies, sparrows, dogs and gorillas. While other animals like being alone, such as blue herons, cats and orangutans. Humans are social animals."

He was right, they were social animals, and it was while standing there at the window that he made love to her again. After which, he asked her more questions and it was this time she chose not to answer, and it was this time he chose to accept her silence. She later saw him writing more in his journal, detailing the silences of a woman, she supposed.

It gave her satisfaction to be with him. He wanted to make-believe he was Aristotle, and she decided to make-believe it for one night the way many one-nighters believe in love for one night. She wasn't actually sure whether they spent one night or an entire weekend together because their time with each other was blurred.

"Time is made up of moments," he told her. And

then he asked, "How do you define a moment?" and before she could reply, he answered his own question. "A moment is a degree of reality."

In their degrees of reality, there was lovemaking, or perhaps she should refer to it as sex-making, because she knew what real lovemaking was. There was falling asleep, waking up, more sex-making, eating and drinking, and lots and lots of talking. They passionately analyzed each other's thoughts and spoke in syllogisms—mastering structures of sentences that could meaningfully be called true or false. She was able to debate his opinions in politics and ethics and poetry. Whenever they held a difference of opinion, he would write down her views. Whenever they agreed, he found no reason to record a thing. The majority of these events happened in bed. Discussion was played like a chess game where their minds were their joint chessboard and the pawns, knights, bishops, rooks, queens and kings were their words.

He never once bragged about himself, but he did say that most people considered him to be a natural born scholar and that Plato had nicknamed him, "The Brain." She worried that he took himself far too seriously in playing the role of Aristotle when they both knew he was not. He, however, continued speaking as if he was the greatest thinker who ever lived.

Passionate and compassionate, though, he asked, "Are you ready to ask me the question you came all this way for?"

She told him she didn't have a question anymore.

"Please. What was the question you asked of all your beacons along the way? What was your question for Aristotle?"

"I'm not looking for an answer anymore. Every single time I've asked the question, I've received the opposite of what I wanted."

"Well then, allow me to pose my query differently. What was the definitive answer you received to your question?"

"An array of never-ending, confusing answers containing nothing more than mixed messages. All answers offered virtually the same result: nothing but a void that goes on and on and on. And that, I suspect, is the answer in itself."

"One should never give up on what one most wants. Do you think I'm ever going to give up on what I want?"

"No."

"Tell me, what mixed messages did you receive?"

"Well, for example, one person told me 'change is illusion' and another person told me 'only change is real.'"

"You have Aristotle all to yourself, now. What you need to do is ask me the question."

She hesitated.

"I see your problem quite clearly. If you want a true answer to your question, you cannot, under any circumstances, be wary of your true answer. You are too attached to the result of your question. Any scientist would go mad if he cherished any question as personally as you have done."

Her face felt strained, she didn't know what to say or do at this point. She couldn't have felt hollower.

"For the degree of reality in which we are together, allow me to help you. What was it that brought you all this way?"

"You would probably laugh."

"And what if I did? Again, you are too emotionally attached to the result of your question. If you want the truth, you must be bold. If you want only one answer and one answer alone, I'm afraid all the probabilities and statistics in the world will grant you great disappointment."

She held onto her silence until he filled it. "The ultimate value of life depends upon awareness and the power of contemplation rather than upon mere survival."

It was then she decided, why not. What did she have to lose asking her question of a womanizer who wanted her to believe he was Aristotle? It would be absurd for her to hold back at this point. She decided to tell him everything, and while she spoke, he listened to her without a fragment of distraction.

She told him she knew what Real Love was and that she had lost Real Love. She told him she wanted to know that she would see Real Love again. She told him what The Tourist had said about Aristotle and that it was his fault she would never know. She told him she had come to Athens to see Aristotle's excavations, but there was nothing there but rubble and then a woman in a taxi told her about Plato's Academe. She told him that when she arrived at Plato's Academe, she met an Old Greek Man who told her she needed to sleep. She told him about her New Friend who taught her that music was the key to everything and about The Priestess who told her to be thankful for everything but that the leaves of the Oak Tree did not speak to her. She told him about The Italian who took her to meet The Goddess of Truth. She told him she hitchhiked and that The Valiant Men,

The Driver and The Passenger, took her to The Agora for a Kledones, where she also did not receive a clear answer. And she told him people seemed to know who The Driver and The Passenger were; they seemed to have a following and that the younger one, The Driver, had given her a gold coin that she used to get to Trophonius and that Trophonius was far too dark. It was after being placed on the Throne of Memory too many times that she tried to end her life, and that's when a spirit of some sort saved her life and then at the river there was a boy who quoted the words of Heraclitus.

"And then I met you," she explained.

There was silence between them until he filled it again. "I don't understand about my excavations. What of rubble? Where was this?"

"I don't know exactly where. It was somewhere in Athens."

"Not Aristotle's Lyceum?"

"What used to be Aristotle's Lyceum."

"That can't be!"

"As sure as I am sitting here, I was there and Aristotle's Lyceum was being excavated. That's all I can tell you."

She could see he didn't believe her.

He overlooked the entire notion of excavations and continued with their primary discussion. "And what was the question you asked of all these men and women and Priestesses and Goddesses and Oracles along the way?"

"Will I ever see him again? I believe I will, but I want to know."

"And do you know it now? Or do you not know it now?"

"Time and circumstance commanded me to give up. Yes, I wanted to know it, but I was not given the gift of such knowledge. It was exactly in that degree of reality of giving up when I met you. The man who calls himself Aristotle."

His mind continued to mull over her question. He persisted, "You say you want to know about Real Love but what you really mean to say is that you want to know that there is life after death."

"Yes, I suppose."

"May I strongly suggest that you say the sentence aloud so that you understand what it is you are asking?"

"I don't understand what you mean."

"Please say: I want to know that there is life after death."

"Ok, I want to know that there is life after death."

That's when he laughed. Deep and without words, his laugh contained a variety of syllables and notes. Then he said, "My dear, the sentence is a contradiction in itself. It makes no sense."

"A lot of people believe it, I want to know it. Or I wanted to know it. Maybe I don't even know what I want anymore."

"People who believe in Life After Death are emotional. Willful and ignorant."

"So you don't believe any human can come back after dying?"

"Believing is far from the point. Intellect makes us human and the only thing that survives death is intellect. Sure, your New Friend Pythagoras, and your Italian Parmenides, your Passenger Socrates, who non-coincidentally was also your One-In-The-Same

Old Greek Man in the Park, and even your Driver Plato toyed around with the idea of recycled souls or reincarnation at one time. They all failed to prove it. For logic to work, it must have a literal meaning and things literally can only be true or false. Otherwise, all things that cannot be considered true or false fall into the category of not making sense, i.e. nonsense. Therefore, once nonsense is struck from conceptual thinking, the idea of Life after Death becomes merely a contradiction. And nonsense, as you have now concluded, is no longer applicable."

"And the Oracles?" she hated to ask.

"Sorrow, pain and delusion set a great stage for an Oracle to appear and tell you everything is the way you want it to be. And if the Oracles were in fact truth, above all our knowing or understanding, why would something so wise and so pure cost money?"

She quoted what The Driver had said to her, "Reason can only take you so far, sometimes truth has to come down and set you aflame."

"Yes, Your Driver Plato was dear to you and dear to me, but dearer still is the truth. Plato was far too emotional; in his degree of reality he could have outlived us all, he could have been the most brilliant man ever. But his personal attachments, including that of, if not especially to, Socrates, stood in his way. And then our dear Plato taught Aristotle until he could teach Aristotle no more."

"I believe there might be a flaw in your thinking."

"I beg your pardon?"

"Well for example, I've seen Aristotle's excavations and you haven't. You don't believe me, but I know it as a fact. Can you not know something even though you've not seen it? Can you know anything even if you'll never lay your eyes on it? I can prove Aristotle's excavations, and you cannot. So is this another case of illogical thinking? To you, such a thing as Aristotle's excavations is nonsense. And to me, it is completely true."

This disturbed him deeply, yet he retained his focus. "I am not afraid of the answer of whether or not there are Aristotle's excavations. If I want the truth, I will find it. You, on the other hand, continue to be afraid of your answer. You will never do anything in this world without courage. It is the greatest quality of the mind next to honor."

"Some people along the way have said I do, in fact, embody courage and boldness."

"What other people may say of you or think of you is not the point. Hurray if others see courage and boldness in you. But what if someone believes in you and you don't have the truth inside to align with his or her views? Do you live off what other people think of you, or are you courageous every time you take a step? Courageous, not because someone else says you are, or thinks you are, or believes you are. You are courageous because you and you alone silently say to yourself ceaselessly, I have the veracious courage to uncover the truth, whatever the answer may hold. If you do this with each door you open, on the other side of every entrance or exit truth and truth alone awaits you. Without that internal courage, you are more than likely to experience a variety of mind disorders. And the energy of the mind is the essence of life."

Before she could respond, he finalized, "Trepidation and courage cannot exist side by side. True, they may take turns like a swinging door, but fear and courage can never live under the same roof."

"If you are Aristotle, for sure you are brilliant. You created the science of logic, you in fact helped create the template for all future sciences that future societies will use."

"Get not your friends by bare compliments, but by giving them sensible tokens of your love." All this was said as he pulled her closer.

"Is that an Aristotle quote?"

"Socrates, in fact, said it best."

"After creating logic, what if there was just one flaw, and you happened to be wrong. Wouldn't you want to set the world straight? Liberate us from the constraints of the mind, and acknowledge that there are greater things at play? Knowing there is a greater truth rather than relying on the limitations of the human brain?"

He was worried for a fleeting moment, then became fortified with himself again.

He didn't laugh, he smiled. He examined her more and scribbled down a few more notes. When he put away his notepad, he reached out to her again, pulling her in closely.

Would it be more sex-making or might this transform into lovemaking, she was wondering. He held her more passionately than before, when there was a clamoring outside the door.

He stood up abruptly, only offering three words. "Excuse me, dear." He left her alone inside his bedroom.

She waited for him underneath the tangled sheets, understanding she would need to leave soon. There was nothing for her here. Yes, there was a man who wanted her to believe he was Aristotle who comforted her, and she was the anonymous woman who comforted him. But this was not Real Love. He had helped her accept that Real Love was gone, and he had helped her learn there were many things in life other than the pursuit of Real Love.

Was the man who called himself Aristotle right? Was she too emotionally attached to the answer to her own question? Yes of course she was. It didn't take a philosopher to tell her that. Weren't all obsessions result-oriented?

She then remembered The Priestess and decided to thank all there ever was for every single thing that happened, Before Real Love, During Real Love, the Loss of Real Love and After Real Love and all Her Guides and for the mythological Oracles. And now, even for acknowledgment of her result-oriented obsession. And her newly acquired skill of sex-making. Sex-making without love highlighted the intellect and the physical, and magnified loneliness. For sex without love was another frontier altogether, a place she imagined she would go every so often, but hoped would never be her true destination. She was thankful for all the unraveling of truths, even truths she did not understand.

Her personal degree of reality was preparing herself to return, getting ready to depart, when another woman entered the bedroom. A jealous lover had arrived speaking rapidly in Greek, and it did not surprise her that a womanizer would deliver such a circumstance. She told the Jealous Lover not to worry, she would be leaving and would not return. The man who called himself Aristotle observed, with a sparkle in his eye.

The Jealous Lover kept aggressively talking at her and to him. She couldn't really tell who the Jealous Lover was more upset with. All the while, the man who wanted her to believe he was Aristotle helped her get re-dressed. He delicately re-wrapped her in the white linen shroud and walked her to the door. He started to open the door for her, but she wanted to open the door herself, and she did so, no longer un-afraid but with courage.

He stood under the threshold with her, offering, "It is rare that I am surprised. Most women become too attached to me and you have not. Why is that?"

She answered, "You will always be the one who taught me not to get too attached to the questions of life and instead to embrace the answers. Your answer is here, mine is out there somewhere."

In their degree of reality, he seemed to be moved. There was something between them; if it was love, it was a different kind of love, not Real Love. That did not discount what they had together from being authentic.

He asked, "I have one last question, if you will?"

"I will."

"Were you faithful to your husband?"

"We were never married although I called him my husband, and he called me his wife. And yes, we were faithful not because we were supposed to be, but be-cause we wanted to be. And now I have one last ques-tion for you, if you will."

"I will," he said.

"Will you get married someday?"

"I don't know, but if I were to marry, I would be faithful because that's what husbands do. You know what your Old Man in the Park and One-In-The-Same

Passenger advised men on the subject of marriage, don't you?"

She didn't know.

He answered his own question: "Socrates' advice to man was this: By all means get married. If you find a good wife you will be happy; if not, you will become a philosopher."

The Jealous Lover witnessed their exchange and although she didn't understand their words, she understood something important had transpired between them, which only increased her hostility.

She observed the Jealous Lover's tears and understood them so well: the want of something that no longer is. She reminded herself, "Only change is real."

The man who called himself Aristotle returned to his Jealous Lover and she closed the door behind her, re-entering her personal wilderness again. She would return to Athens and she would return home. Whatever home would be to her when she got there was another matter, but she was ready to return. She believed she had her answer, knowing she would never know. Just like The Old Man in the Park had told her might wind up being the case.

But first she had to get out of the building she was in. She wasn't sure whether she was in an upscale apartment complex or an understated hotel. She didn't even remember arriving at the residence of the man who wanted to be known as Aristotle. The only thing she remembered was having been there.

CHAPTER THIRTY

WHITEWASHED CORRIDORS and other closed off private rooms were all that could be seen in front of and behind her. A symphony of the unknown was the soundtrack. The only thing she could hear was the muffled sound of a vacuum cleaner playing her a love-song. The artless and vacant hallways reverberated with the cleaning machine's harmony while she tried her best not to concentrate on Real Love or loneliness. She tried to replace all thoughts with thankfulness. She tried thanking God or The Gods or The Goddess or The Goddesses for her lost weekend with the man who wanted to be known as Aristotle. But then she told the Deities she had made a mistake, "No, I do not wish to thank you all, whatever you are, for a Lost Weekend. I wish to thank you all for a Weekend Gained."

None of the private doorways and passageways she tried, opened. They were all locked, firmly closed. And none of the corridors led to an exit. The immaculate white walls and floors seemed to have the same historic palette of marble and stone as the palace where The Italian Parmenides had taken her to meet The Goddess. She thought back to The Goddess and her translucent skin. But then did Goddesses in general have skin, or did they merely illuminate images of flesh?

And when she thought more about The Goddess, all that she had taught her in song, she remembered some of the verse and then she sang aloud, "Altering bright colors." Her meek voice traveled the empty hallways, "Everything that is, always has been and always will be. You've, I've, been on this road many times. Only one story, only one road, only now is left."

When she finished singing the song was exactly when The Goddess appeared right in front of her.

She was not startled or surprised to see The Goddess. She enthusiastically told her, "After I met you, I was hitchhiking and then Two Valiant Men picked me up and they told me your name was Aletheia and that you taught the wisdom of truth to The Italian, Parmenides. And if it weren't for you, truth wouldn't exist today."

The Goddess of Truth, Aletheia, asked her only one question. "You are ready to return?"

"Yes."

"You received the wisdom you came for?"

"I did not get what I came for, but I accept the wisdom I have received."

"You have one last task that will take you back. Are you ready, no matter what it is you might find?"

"I'm well beyond ready."

The Goddess Aletheia instructed her to choose a door and then to open it.

"I've tried all the doors here. Every single one of

them and they are all locked. I've tried every passage-way and there are no exits."

"What about an entrance?" The Goddess Aletheia questioned.

"I've seen none."

"And what are you standing on?"

"Well, I'm standing on a white bright floor, with many winding paths. Each and every passage here leads to nothing."

"Everything you need is right where you are."

"I want to believe that, I really do, but the Truth is Aletheia, I'm not experiencing that."

"Regard. What is just below the soles of your feet?"

She took a small step backward and saw that she had been standing atop a white doorway, leading downward. The Goddess waited for her to reach her hand toward the doorknob below. When she did this, the door below opened automatically, revealing a shaft of darkness.

She asked The Goddess, "Have I not been through enough darkness?"

The answer she received was, "And were you not ready to return before?"

She observed The Goddess Aletheia more closely. She was less radiant than before, although she still embodied beauty. She seemed like she could have been a close friend or a sister. Aletheia held out a small stone and instructed, "Now, you will hold this in the palm of your hand and when you are ready, you will throw this stone over your shoulder. This act will symbolize leaving your past behind. Do you understand?"

"Yes, I believe I do understand."

"And will you do this?"

She nodded, "Yes, I will."

The Goddess Aletheia then placed the stone inside the palm of her left hand. She clasped it tightly, then descended down an incline and when she reached the bottom of the basement floor, the ceiling above was too low for her to remain standing. There was only one passage forward, and so she was forced to crawl on her hands and knees, holding the stone tightly. She looked up and saw that The Goddess would not be coming with her and then with a sincere heart, she thanked Aletheia. And then The Goddess of Truth closed the door from above and she was in complete darkness again. With courage and a stone, she crawled forward, and when she was ready, she did as The Goddess had instructed her.

She unclasped her hand, and the stone glistened in the dark. She held onto it for a while, embracing the notion that her past was actually in the palm of her hand. And then she did it. She threw the stone over her shoulder just as The Goddess had told her to do. She left her past behind. With this simple act, she felt much freer than she had ever expected. As if the past, present and future came together entirely into one single moment, one degree of reality that offered the sensation that anything was possible. Simply everything created of beauty was possible.

Both her pericardium and her heart enlivened. And suddenly lanterns and torches lit up the one passageway ahead. She saw women of all ages, all races, standing tall, holding the lighted flames high so that she could find her way. Whether they were Goddesses or Mothers or Sisters or Daughters, she did not know.

She stood up amongst them and walked down her one road very quickly. Confusion was replaced by clarity, one passage after the other. More welcoming females, dignitaries, guided her at every turn. She was not lost or remotely afraid anymore; she was going somewhere filled with strength and courage. And she soon noticed that none of these women had caught her eye. The women either bowed their heads down or looked above toward the heavens. At first she didn't understand but then she soon caught on. It was out of respect that they were not looking directly at her. Something ahead of her was so personal and significant that the rows of women did not want to influence its outcome.

And then she entered a small circular chamber where another woman greeted her without words. Two more women carried antique pitchers filled with well water and poured the fresh water into the giant bronze caldron in the center of the room. After which, another woman came into the room carrying a crystal pitcher filled with virgin olive oil. She poured this fresh oil atop the water's surface. The women then ceremoniously placed a dozen flaming torches inside the chamber and then closed the passageway behind them. Not one of them had given her any instruction on what to do. In fact, none had spoken a word.

She stood inside the lighted room alone. The open flames gave off intense heat but she did not feel hot. Instinctively, she moved to look inside the caldron and saw the most beautiful image of the room reflecting back at her. The mirrored images from the caldron made the circular room appear to be twice its size and it reflected so much light back into the chamber, she felt that the sun itself had somehow come down just to be with her.

She then looked deeper into the reflective waters. She, of course, could see herself. And that image alone brought to her eyes a dampness. Once again, past, present and future all in the same moment made her feel an emotional high and low. The elation of being alive was filled with altering bright colors just as the hallways and corridors had been and just as The Goddess Aletheia had once described, but not altering bright because someone told her so, but because she was experiencing it so. Whatever came next, she not only was ready for it, she wanted it. And courage had little to do with it.

CHAPTER THIRTY-ONE

SHE CONTINUED TO STARE into the caldron's reflective waters, waiting and waiting for something to happen. She was not gazing at herself, she was gazing at the mirrored images of the golden circular room that were nothing less than mesmerizing.

And soon, it began to rain into the bronze bowl of water. There were no clouds and it was not falling from the sky because she, of course, was below ground level. Nor was the precipitation coming from the ceiling. And then she realized the rain was coming from her eyes. But she was not sad. Her personal rain dropped delicately into the caldron and the waves of her tears atop the oil caused a minor current to ripple across the water. Again, she experienced the elation of being fully alive in which the measurement of time had no meaning.

And then she saw another image. This time, it was of him. At long last, the face of Real Love was gazing up at her from inside the bronze caldron.

Her first instinct was that it was true; Real Love was there with her. And then within the dimension of a second, her mind's instinct was that it was absolutely not him. Her loneliness up to this point must have generated a mirage of hope that manifested Real Love's imagery in order to see him. These were thoughts and not facts. These were the insights that the man who wanted to be known as Aristotle had shared with her. She remembered his words well, "People who believe in Life After Death are emotional. Willful and ignorant."

She closed her eyes tight, her mind's attempt to convince itself that she could not see Real Love. Yet when she reopened her eyes, his image remained. She splashed her hands into the pool of water, trying to make sense of it, or perhaps trying to get rid of it, but Real Love's image never wavered.

She remembered words of doubt once again, "Sorrow, pain and delusion set a great stage for an Oracle to appear and tell you everything is the way you want it to be."

She spoke back to the empty chamber, to the mirage of Real Love and to the voice of doubt, "I did not ask to see my dead love in a caldron of oil and water. I did not create this illusion."

She moved away from the caldron and pondered what the truth was. It was Aletheia, The Goddess of Truth, who had brought her here. According to The Valiant Men, Aletheia invented truth, or created it. Or maybe, she thought, maybe Aletheia simply was truth and that truth was never created; it always was and always will be. Truth, she imagined, never changes. Only a woman's or a man's perception of truth changes.

And then she heard Real Love's voice. He responded to her inner turbulence as if she had spoken those feelings aloud. "You are correct. Truth never changes. And Real Love never dies."

And yet his image was no longer residing inside the caldron. It was his voice. She was sure of it, and his voice was as clear and audible as if he were there with her. And then she looked up and saw his entire image on the other side of the chamber. There, Real Love was. Standing tall, dressed exactly as he had been on his last day. His checkered shirt, top button missing, his old blue jeans and his ancient black loafers. His clothes and shoes, hair and skin, his entire being was soaking wet. Water dripped from the image of Real Love, just as if he had come out of the river on the day of his death and never drowned. But an image couldn't fool her. She knew he had drowned and that he was dead. So why was Real Love's image standing in front of her, her mind wondered? He was much too far away for being in such a confined space. His image stepped around the caldron and moved toward her. He placed his two arms around her and without words, he held her and she held him back.

And, love was real again. It was not only his image, she could feel him. His arms and his body, his mind, his eyes radiated Real Love once again, as golden as the chamber they were in. She breathed him in while they held onto each other—and everything up until now made no sense, yet it all seemed true.

"Love never dies," he repeated.

"But you are really not here, you are an image."

"All the philosophers were right in their own way. Yes, change is illusion and only change is real. Truth doesn't change and bodies decay and love never dies."

She stared at him in disbelief. Wanting to know,

but not capable of such a feat.

"Haven't you felt me the entire time?" Real Love asked.

"Yes, I thought maybe, but I wanted to know it."

"And do you know it now?"

"I'm not sure."

"Even when Real Love is standing in front of you, holding you, you are not sure?"

"I'm sorry. Being left alive, with you gone. Your absence is the most devastating thing that's ever happened or ever will happen."

"Yet I've been with you silently the whole time."

"There was no real proof."

"Can anyone ever prove love while they are living, let alone after they are gone?"

She didn't offer an answer.

He asked, "Isn't it when I was still alive, that you knew love? As I recall, you didn't believe in it, you knew love. Even amongst the living, hardly a soul believes in love anymore, let alone knows it. Husbands suspect their wives, wives suspect their husbands. Doubts between lovers, family, friends and colleagues happen every single moment somewhere in the world without the separation of death."

"Doubt in each other was never our problem."

"Truth," was all he said.

"And your apparition now, will I be more devastated when your image goes away or will I continue to find a new strength to go on without you?"

"But I am not an apparition, I am as real as I ever was and you have never been without me. You've been too busy trying to believe the truth rather than accepting that you actually know the truth."

As much as she wanted it, *to know*, the possibility was more overwhelming than she imagined it would be.

"You have known the answer the entire time—you just haven't believed it."

"Prove it," she challenged him.

"Never cut flowers."

"You know about Never Cut Flowers and Trophonius?"

"In our lives together, didn't I always give you uncut flowers? Never a dozen cut blossoms of any kind. Only plants of orchids and roses. Why do you think?"

She didn't answer because, she knew.

"Everybody knows roses die during the winter and then somehow, beyond our comprehension they come back to life in the spring again. And they keep coming back year after year. We know this without rationale and yet it is considered a certainty because we've witnessed it."

She quoted the man who wanted to be known as Aristotle, "Natures does nothing uselessly."

"We are nature, are we not? Orchids have a growth period and a resting period. If we can learn anything from them, other than pure beauty, might we say that I am resting and that you are growing?"

She wanted him to be right, but could that prove he was really there? Or was everything she ever wanted playing itself out in her mind?

"Who stopped you from taking your own life prematurely? Who pulled you from the river?"

She looked at him. She had felt a presence when she was pulled from the river, although she couldn't prove that it was he and she couldn't prove that it was not he. She confessed, "I would have pulled you from the Hudson River if I could have."

"It doesn't matter."

"It does. Maybe Aristotle was right—sorrow can create an image of what we want to believe."

"That is true sometimes. Aristotle's theories are right most of the time. But there were other times when he was wrong. Didn't Aristotle believe, for example, that the earth was the center of the universe and that the stars, the sun and the moon revolved around the earth? Yet we all know the earth revolves around the sun."

She stood silently in his arms while he continued, "And, he disregarded intuition altogether. What would any universe be without a woman's intuition?"

"Or a man's intuition?" she quietly added.

"Unwavering truth is stronger than any belief."

She breathed him in and then whispered, "Truth always was and always will be."

"And love that is true, always was and always will be," he whispered back to her.

"Real Love," she surrendered.

"You know I am here, don't you?"

And with everything that ever mattered to her, she answered, "Yes, I know."

They held each other close. Far closer and far more intimately than when he was living. The energy of his being was inhaled and exhaled throughout her being as if golden light from the chamber had entered both their bodies and had swirled them into one. Seemingly beyond this world and beyond any ethereal world, it was happening in their world. Love and truth and knowing created a transparent shield protecting the two of them. She felt quite possibly that they were one being. One thing. Was love one thing? Whatever love was, whatever this state of being was, whatever dimension they might be in, she never wanted it to end. And before she knew it, Real Love's hair and skin, his clothes and shoes were all dry as if he never dove into the river that day.

"No one will believe me," she sighed.

"We never worried about what other people thought when I was living, why should we worry now?"

"But I want everyone to know."

"And when people don't believe you, it won't make you feel lost or uncertain again?"

"Nothing can take the truth away now. Nothing."

"And if skeptics mock you and say you are delusional, or if they call you a fanatic, that won't hurt you? Frustrate you?"

"I would try to explain it to them. All of it."

"If anyone had told you the truth, would you have believed them or would you have wanted to find out on your own?"

He was right, she had needed to discover this—the affirmation of knowing on her own. With all her beacons along the way, helping, guiding and contradicting, she had to claim this knowledge within herself. "So then we won't tell a soul?"

"Not unless they ask."

The peacefulness between them kept them protected and warm. Their inner strength together could thus shatter any obstacle, even that of death.

She hesitated to ask, but posed the question anyway, "What next?"

"I'll be with you until you are ready to return."

"So when will we see each other again?"

"I suppose after you grow and I rest, we will re-unite again."

"But how does it work?"

"I don't claim to understand how, I just know. We just know, don't we?"

"Will we have to wait one year or a thousand? How will we find each other?"

"Just like we found each other before, we will find each other again. And in the interval, however long that lasts, live life well for the both of us."

"Without you?"

"Fully and courageously just as you have done so far. I am proud of you."

In their measurement of time and in their degree of reality, they continued to hold each other. Words were no long necessary. She didn't know whether it was days, hours, seconds, minutes, years or exactly how many moments they held each other. There was no hurry to move forward, no eagerness to take a step back, no action or thought or task was considered. They just were.

And together they listened to the chamber music playing the refrain of the flickering torches. They listened to the past, to the present and to the future as being one thing. Knowing one thing. Love like truth, is, was and always will be.

Real Love unwavering and complete.

CHAPTER THIRTY-TWO

RAYS OF THE SUN danced across her body. She kept her eyes closed for a while longer, lingering in the state of euphoria where time doesn't exist and Real Love does. And then she opened her eyes.

A young man stared at her from above, an unfamiliar bright face that spoke, "Hope is a waking dream."

Realization immediately set in that Real Love was no longer there. Her equilibrium was off and her whereabouts were disorienting, and it was all the stranger because somehow she had returned to the empty park—Plato's Academe. She was lying on the ancient stones just where The Old Greek Man had left her. She could see that she was fully dressed again, no longer wrapped in a white linen shroud and no longer barefoot. She was wearing the same clothes she had worn to Plato's Academe that first day. Dressed in a simple blouse and trousers, comfortable walking shoes, and she still had her handbag with her—all its contents were still there. She could hear the sound of Athens. The Young Man offered his hand, but she got up on her own.

She was lightheaded and asked, "Is The Old Greek Man still here?"

The Young Man clearly didn't know who she was talking about.

She told him, "An Old Greek Man gave me a tour of Plato's Academe and told me all about the history of this park, and then he suggested I lie down in this exact spot and that I needed to dream."

The Young Man could only offer, "I've not seen anyone here today, other than you."

"And you are?"

"Guardian of the park, for two years now. It's a fairly easy job because it's a forgotten place that no one usually comes to and if they do, they don't stay for very long."

"How long was I lying down on these stones? Do you know?"

He shrugged. "Twenty minutes, maybe a half hour."

"And you didn't see an Old Man or a Homeless Man come into the park today?"

He shook his head, no. He then pointed over to a ditch in the ground and told her, "That used to be Plato's olive tree, right over there. Planted by Plato himself."

She then told him, "Until a tour bus hit it and the olive tree was taken away for experimentation, to prove what everybody already knew. It was Plato's tree."

"How did you know that?"

She explained again about The Old Greek Man and what he had told her, but the Young Man didn't quite believe her. She thanked him anyway and then walked back across the grounds of the most unremarkable-looking park she had ever been to, heading out the same way she had entered.

At the edge of Plato's park, she felt a prickling or a tingling inside the front pocket of her blouse. She reached inside her pocket and pulled out a twig laden with tiny white blossoms along its branch. The very twig that The Italian, Parmenides, had given her before introducing her to The Goddess of Truth. Aletheia, she thought back. She was thankful and grateful for Aletheia and for all things.

She looked across her one road ahead, just as it was before. And the sun was positioned high and scorching, just as it was before. While she waited for another agricultural truck to go by before crossing, she noticed the old worn-out shoe in the middle of the road. No vehicle had yet run over it. The traffic became clear again and all sounds of the 21st Century evaporated just as before. As she walked across her silent road and on passing the old shoe, she heard the same audible voice reprising, *"Whenever you see one abandoned shoe on its own, it indicates that someone has left one world, and has entered another."*

She crossed to the other side where she saw, just up ahead, what appeared to be the same taxi she had taken earlier that day. The same Taxi Driver was parked on the side of the road where he had stopped to take a break and was eating his lunch. She moved to the Taxi Driver's window.

"Can you take me back to my hotel, and then can you wait for me? I would like to go collect my things and then I would like to head straight to the airport. Please."

"Going home so soon?" the Taxi Driver asked.

"Yes, I found what I was looking for."

The Taxi Driver started his automobile's engine again and she placed herself in the back seat next to the dirty passenger window. She held onto the white-blossomed twig as the taxi drove her away. And just like before, as they merged back onto the disorderly streets of Athens, some of the roads were bumpy, while others were smooth, and the noise of the city was pitched at a high level. Massive drillings in roads, too much traffic and blaring car radios, buses and fumes. The same chaos as was before as the taxi moved through the city.

The Taxi Driver asked, "What did you find that you had to come all this way for, may I ask?"

She thought about it before she answered, "Love is a single soul inhabiting two bodies."

"So then, you found Aristotle?"

"No, I researched Aristotle in a library back in New York, I must have remembered that quote from one of the books I read."

"Well, not everything Aristotle said was true."

"Truth," she grinned.

The Taxi Driver continued through a variety of major streets and side streets of the city. He only asked her one more question, which was, "So, do you believe you will see him again?"

"Him?"

"Real Love. Do you believe you'll see him again?"

She took in a deep breath and then answered, "No, I don't believe I'll see him again. I know it."

He nodded his head in a traditional Greek way, subtle. It wasn't clear whether she met his approval or disapproval. Either way, he was kind and on the brief intersection of their one road together, their journey was a pleasant one.

She tried once again to roll down the passenger window and then quickly remembered it would not roll down any farther. She looked out the broken window, past the filth and the smudge and then saw through the dirt that prisms of golden light were filtering into the taxi. A kaleidoscope of altering bright colors and warmth. She held the blossomed twig delicately as they continued through the city of Athens. And she didn't need to remind herself that love, like truth, is, was and always will be. She knew it.

The noise of the traffic played like a symphony. She listened to her personal soundtrack with the street drills drumming and the car horns trumpeting. She was ready to return and was not in a hurry, knowing she would be grateful for the sound of life for as long as it lasted.

AFTERWORD

THE ANCIENT GREEK philosophers who founded logic and reason also set the ground rules for thinking about spiritual life. These early philosophers studied near-death experiences, journeyed to the after-death world, and called up spirits of the deceased. In fact, logic itself began at an early Greek oracle of the dead. And as a result practically every Western person constantly carries these philosophers around and continually puts their philosophical principals to use in the transactions of everyday life. This is especially so of the five colorful characters portrayed in this book: Pythagoras, Parmenides, Socrates, Plato and Aristotle.

Pythagoras, born on the Greek island of Samos around 570 BCE, traveled throughout the Greek world consulting oracles and trying to decipher how they worked. Squeezed out of his homeland by political developments, he fled to the Greek City of Croton in Southern Italy. There he built an astonishing educational center that was the first institution of higher learning in the Western world.

Pythagoras' school consisted of a subterranean

chamber where students isolated themselves for long periods in total darkness. No doubt they had visionary experiences, which they took to be visits to the world beyond death. Above ground, students assembled in a music hall to listen to lectures and to practice a startling form of therapy where musical tones were used to heal various mental or physical afflictions. Numbers were the centerpiece of Pythagoras' teaching. He discovered the mathematical structure of nature, the doctrine that still underlies modern science. Yet this pillar of scientific thought was profoundly mystical in its inception.

Pythagoras was as much a mystic, religious visionary and inspirational spiritual leader as he was a rational thinker. Indeed, reason was not clearly separate from religion at that time. That separation was a modern development. However, it began with a second-generation student of Pythagorean ideas, Parmenides of Elea. Elea was a Greek City in Southern Italy near modern-day Naples. Parmenides was a prophet-physician at a local oracle of the dead.

Parmenides isolated himself in an oracular cave and visited the other world by the process of dream incubation. He would lie stock still in total darkness, a practice that induced a profound visionary state. In about 500 BCE during one of his visionary voyages to the other side, Parmenides met a Goddess. This Goddess sang him a song—the very first, written-out logical deductive argument. The Goddess instructed Parmenides to take the song back to the land of the living. Parmenides encouraged his students to sing the Goddess' song over and over until they learned it by heart. When they did, the students came to understand that some statements are anchored in reality in a way that was independent of any particular person's belief or perception. This is the quality that today we know was truth. So in a very real sense, Parmenides was the person who first propounded the notion of independent truth. And that concept is the basis of the system of logic we still use today, not just in scientific and academic thought but in thinking about problems of daily life.

These earlier philosophers mostly made statements and proposed arguments in favor of their own positions. The Athenian Socrates (469–399 BCE) was the first philosopher to explore how questions work. He first achieved fame as a war hero, showing valor in a battle in which his fellow soldiers panicked and fled. At this period, he was apparently a swaggering braggart and perhaps also somewhat of a dirty old man as he aged. Nonetheless, he developed an intense interest in the big questions of existence. At first, he studied what we would today call natural science—questions about the heavens, the moon and the sun and so on. Eventually however, Socrates became interested in ethical concepts of virtue and happiness. He went around Athens questioning anyone who claimed to have knowledge about ethical concerns.

Socrates soon realized that those who had pretensions to knowledge about ethics did not really have it. He found he could make these pretentious individuals contradict themselves with just a few of his probing questions. Naturally, this created a great deal of resentment in Athens and when Socrates was seventy years old, the city put him on trial. Many Athenians believed that Socrates called up the spirits of the dead. Rightly or wrongly, that was one of the main things ordinary citizens had against him. Indeed, they believed that a philosopher was someone who practiced evocation of ghosts. Whether or not that was true of Socrates, it was definitely true of some philosophers of that period.

Socrates lived his life in near-poverty with little interest in material wealth. Yet as the inventor of the art of cross-examination and the first person to insist on clear definitions, Socrates is an enduring presence in daily life in the West. He also lives on through his immense influence on his most famous pupil, the man who established the university system as we still know it.

This student, Aristocles, was a very sensitive man who was also a rugged, muscular professional wrestler. So we know him today by his ring name: Plato. Plato was devastated by his teacher Socrates' trial, conviction and execution. During what seems to have been a deep midlife crisis and perhaps coming to terms with his homosexuality, Plato traveled abroad. Then, returning to Athens he purchased a property near the city. The facility consisted of a gymnasium and other buildings Plato used as dormitory rooms, lecture halls, dining areas and a library. This institution was the prototype for all subsequent universities. And since it was in a grove of trees known as academe, the place gave its name to academia as we have it today in a continuing tradition.

Plato divided the world into sensible and intelligible spheres. He gave very little credence to the sensible, physical world of ever-changing phenomena. Rather, Plato focused his attention to the changeless, timeless world of intelligible abstract concepts such as goodness and justice, notions that we can only know through our intellect. Plato held out the hope that the physical world is only a small part of the picture and that our true nature lies in a sublime after-death realm free of mortal concerns.

Much of this was lost on Plato's most renowned student Aristotle. Aristotle came to Athens at the age of seventeen years to study at Plato's academy. Plato soon realized that Aristotle was a brilliant thinker with a special talent for logic. Aristotle was fascinated with biology and made a point of collecting specimens of plants and animals and studying animal behavior. In short, Aristotle's mind was bound up in the physical world of ordinary reality.

In the case of Plato and Aristotle, the contrast between teacher and student could not be more stark and dramatic. Plato wrote philosophical plays, dialogues with an impressive dramatic flair. By contrast, Aristotle is remembered for his succinct lecture notes. These notes make up a massive body of work that have shaped Western views of reality for more than two thousand years. Plato's works are abstract and theoretical while Aristotle focused on what is observable to us through our physical senses.

Plato was a somewhat dour and puritanical man who disdained bodily pleasures and had a prudish attitude toward sex. Aristotle was a flashy dresser who sported jewelry and was a notorious womanizer. But when he finally married at age fifty, he remained faithful to his wife. After all, he said, fidelity is what marriage is all about.

More than any other person, Aristotle determined how Western people think. He worked out a code of logic that was so ingenious and powerful that it became the basis of reasoning in all fields of study, including, much later, scientific method. The ultimate effect of that was to deemphasize the spiritual world that had so preoccupied thinkers like Pythagoras, Parmenides, Socrates and Plato. For Aristotle's logic gradually found its way into the thought of ordinary individuals. Finally this logic came to dominate thinking about routine matters of daily life, too.

The West is now poised at a critical state in history. In reality, the only way to get back to our spiritual roots is to retrace our steps and to see how we got to where we are. In doing so, we will have to look at ancient practices known to these early thinkers that created the Western world and its deepest values.

—Raymond A. Moody, Jr. M.D., Ph.D.
Anniston, Alabama

ACKNOWLEDGEMENTS

TO BEGIN, I would like to thank just about everyone I've ever known or come across because everyone, everything, every night and every day influences my writing.

My traveler's eyes were first ignited by my generous mentor and longtime friend Bill Haber, followed by my valiant companions Mat Lundberg and Zack Taylor. But the keys to Greece were a gift from my French brother, Christophe Vessier.

Thank you Christine Howard for reading my first writings all those years ago in Paris and for offering loads of advice whether I took it or not, and for staying the course.

Great uplifters along the way have been a collection of spiritual women, Kim Pentecost, Bobbie Martin, Juliette Lauber and Greek liason, Nancy Biska.

Honorable mention to that gang of East Coast misfits that I call my second family who never failed to encourage and tangibly support. Those being Doug Liman, Avram Ludwig, Liz Hamburg, Roberto De Mitri, Kathryn Marsh, Susan Liebold, Lourdes Liz,

Neal Weisman, Amy Nederlander, David Claessen and Gaby Tana. Exceptionally thankful to Lisa Walborsky who unified in friendship, helped keep my mind, body and spirit in tact.

The writing of this book could not have happened without my elegant dream-championer, Andrew Egan. Appreciative, also, for his and Marta Castrosin's gorgeous book cover design, and for *tous mes amis* at CoolGraySeven, as well as the dear John Melfi.

Thank you to expert Constance Rosenblum for her editing my first draft. Grateful also to the incomparable Naomi Wolf for her vigorous insights and to Colin Robinson for his endless advice; also to Joe Klingler, Sam Fisher, Jimmy McDermott, Nancy Heikin, Terry and Linda Jamison for valued input.

The evolution of words-to-publication would never have manifested without these brilliant women: True friend and gentle warrior, Beth Grossman Makes Things Happen. Indepted also to friend, agent and publisher, Lisa Hagan, whose vision to help change the world one book at a time gave this book its life. Thank you also to Lisa's partner and editor Beth Wareham for her originality and hard work, as well as Laura Smyth for the lovely book layout.

And to the magnificents Dr. Louanne Stratton, Rhonda Stratton and Rochelle Stratton, thank you for leaps of faith and life support.

Thankfulness of the highest order to the best sister and editor in the world Christine Jarosz who at childhood guided me onto the path of Feminism; as well as to the best brother in the world, Phillip Jarosz, who enticed me at an early age to write and to believe in magic. Sending gratitude and love to the other side of the veil to my late brother Steve Jarosz who used to make me laugh like none other and to my late mother Peggy Smith Jarosz who taught me the most important life lesson: Always choose love.

Without question, this book would never have been concieved if it weren't for the profound Dr. Raymond Moody and his fabulous partner in crime, Cheryl Moody. I am deeply thankful to them both, who not only believed in me, but trusted me with Dr. Moody's lifelong research and passion for the Ancient Greek Philosophers. Yet nothing in this book would have been written if it weren't for my real love, Russ Stratton, who took my hand and showed me miraculous worlds I'd never imagined before.

ABOUT THE AUTHOR

JOHANNA BALDWIN is a
writer and producer whose work
includes film, television, theatre
and short stories. *All (Wo)men
Desire To Know* is her debut novel.

Baldwin's short stories and
essays have appeared in numer-
ous publications from *The New
York Times* to *The London Evening
Standard*. One of those stories,
"Her Private Serenade," is featured in the book *More
New York Stories: The Best of the City Section of The New
York Times*.

Her body of work is influenced by her travels
and many homes over the years—from her birthplace
Dallas to Kansas City, Los Angeles, Paris, London and
now New York City. Her greatest inspiration however
comes from individuals and their true stories.

Baldwin began her career as a literary agent at
Creative Artists Agency.

For more information about the author:
www.JohannaBaldwin.com